My Billionaire Benefactor

CANDY GIRLS BOOK 1

SHAE SANDERS

Copyright © 2019 Shae Sanders

Published in the United States of America

Sanders, Shae

My Billionaire Benefactor / Shae Sanders

p. cm.

1. Romance--Fiction

ASIN: B07WVSJK3S (ebook)

ISBN: 9798653805011 (paperback)

First Edition / August 2019

This is a work of fiction. Names, characters, places, and incidents are either a figment of the author's imagination or are used fictitiously, and any resemblance to actual persons, events, or locales is entirely coincidental.

Contents

For all the ladies who get what they want.

1

I'm so broke right now.

It makes no sense. I work for a living. *Two* jobs, if that tells you anything. Well, one and a half, really. And I'm a college girl with a ten-year career plan. I'm not some lazy chick. So how did I get here?

By the way, I'm Imani Princess Emerson. My family and friends call me Imani, Mani, Mon-Mon, and a whole laundry list of other names they think are adorable. At this point, it might be more accurate to call me Loser.

"Hey, when did you say you'd have your half?" Farrah asked, holding up the rental statement. "It's due tomorrow."

I frowned at her from the comfort of my bed. Of course it's due tomorrow. It's always due at the same time every month. Did she think I didn't know that? Although to be fair to her, I think she was trying to say 'bitch better have my money' in a nice way. My bestie is sweet like that.

It was our second year in this place, a cute little two-bedroom on the northern edge of Atlanta. It was Farrah's idea, and I thought it sounded like a nice little adventure. Two grown women doing grown women tings, if you will. But Farrah is slightly more grown than I am, and way better at handling her business. I was floundering. Bad.

"I'll have it. I'm going to see my parents today."

Farrah raised her eyebrows. "You're really gonna ask them? That doesn't sound like you."

"I'm not gonna ask them. I'm gonna inform them of my situation and see if they offer."

My best friend rolled her eyes and shook her head. "I really can't stand you. Just ask them. Or ask *me!*"

I gave her the look. "I don't like asking people for shit. Every time I'm having a hard time, you suggest that to me like we just met. It's really starting to get on my nerves."

"Sorry!" she said as she piled her hair into a bun on top of her head. "Look, I understand...actually, I really don't, but whatever. I wish you would get over that and let people help you sometimes. Believe it or not, it makes other people feel good to help people they love."

She meant well, and I love her for it, but it's so easy for her to say that.

I got dressed and headed out to my parents' house. They live on the east side so it was a bit of a hike. It was hot as balls as July tends to be and the air conditioning in my Civic went out two months ago so you can imagine how much I was suffering. All my windows were down and the wind was blowing nice and strong but I was still a sticky mess when I pulled into their driveway. To make matters worse, I only had a little over a quarter tank of gas. If they didn't offer to help me out, this long drive would be a losing investment.

I rang the bell and was happy when Omari opened the door. My favorite little brother, just five years younger than me and heading into his senior year of high school. In case you're wondering, my other little brother is Giovanni. He's fifteen and I can really take or leave him most days.

Don't even. Everybody has a favorite.

"Mani!" said Omari as he grabbed me in a bear hug. Like all teenage boys, he was musty as hell. I didn't care, though. I buried my face in his chest and squeezed. He was a whole head taller than me and looked like a grown man but inside, he was a little teddy bear.

"How's Daddy?" I asked him.

"He's alright. Just taking it easy. They're out back on the porch."

I gave Omari one last pat on the back before walking toward the back door. My daddy built a screened in sun porch for my mom a few years back and they loved to sit out there and drink lemonade. It was sweet. Whenever I saw them out there together, it made me look forward to the day I find a love like that. If it even still exists.

I took a deep breath and stepped outside. My mom rose immediately. "My baby!" she said as she hugged me. Unlike my brother, my mom doesn't hug hard. She gives church hugs, and it's really cute.

"Hi Mama," I said before kissing her cheek. Her

brown skin was still as smooth as butter. We could be twins, and people often thought we were sisters. The only difference is that she keeps her hair short and I keep mine long.

Despite the huge grin on my daddy's face, he didn't rise to greet me. He'd been nursing a knee injury for months now and on most days, it was hard for him to even use the restroom without help. I leaned down to hug him and smelled his aftershave. "Hi Daddy."

"Well sit on down here," my mother said, pointing to the wicker loveseat. "You want something to eat?"

"No, I just came to see y'all," I said.

Lies.

I had to be careful. I love my mother with all my heart but the woman has the nose of a bloodhound. If my daddy ever sniffed out my bullshit, he kept it to himself. But her? I was in danger, girl.

"So what's going on with you?" she asked, her hackles already raised.

I smiled as innocently as I could and shrugged. "Not much. Just working. School starts back up next month so I'm really looking forward to that. Oh, I tried that recipe you sent me for stuffed manicotti. It was really, really good."

Mama smiled and nodded. "Good, I'm glad you liked it."

"What about y'all? How's your knee, Daddy?"

He mock knocked on his knee and smiled. "Fine. This thing is still hardy. Just aches, is all."

Mama rolled her eyes but said nothing. He was

trying to be strong for me but it didn't keep me from feeling like shit.

"What about you, Mama?" I asked her.

She sighed and glanced at my daddy. "I signed a contract to do a wedding in December," she said, her mouth creeping into a smile.

"Congratulations! That's so exciting. It's been awhile, hasn't it?"

"Almost two years. The only reason I can swing it is because it's a small one. Only fifty people."

I couldn't believe she was finally living her dream. Her wedding planning business had been derailed several times over the years. Most recently, she's had to work a lot more since Daddy's been home recovering. This was a big move for her.

We sat in silence for a while. It wasn't that bad considering we were in a beautiful space, and how could spending time with family not be wonderful? Except I was on a mission and I didn't really have time for all this visiting and whatnot.

Enough was enough. "I'm having a little problem and I wanted to get you guys' advice on it."

Daddy perked up. "What's wrong, Princess?"

Here we go. "Well, my rent is due tomorrow and--"

Mama let out a loud sigh and I jumped.

"--and I just don't have it."

"You have a job. What are you spending your money on?" Mama asked. Her questions always sounded like a police interrogation.

"Nothing, I swear. All of my extra money is in

my school account."

Daddy frowned. "What happened to financial aid?"

"It won't come through until the end of August. Once that kicks in then I'll transfer my school fund money into my checking."

I had been burned before. Sometimes it feels like traditional college students are the priority, not us working folks. I'm a fifth year senior at Georgia State and I've been dropped from my classes enough times to know that I need to have just-in-case money, and it was especially true this year because it will be my last year. It's been a long, hard-fought battle but I will finally be getting my bachelor's degree.

My parents never finished, and their parents never went at all. I'll be the first, and I have my little brothers looking to me as the example. I can't mess this up. I *can't*. My ten-year plan hinges on me graduating in the spring. I'm so close.

Daddy rubbed his salt-and-pepper beard and sighed. "I would love to help you, Mani. I really would."

Uh oh.

"But we're barely getting by. Normally I could still swing it but...I have surgery coming up."

Daddy had been a baggage handler at the airport for almost thirty years before he took extended leave. I'd thought his knee was healing but apparently, I was wrong.

"Wait, surgery? When did you find this out?"

"He didn't wanna worry you," Mama said, her

tone harsh and disapproving.

He stared at the floor. "Sorry, Mani."

I hated that I had even brought it up. The last thing I wanted was to make him feel like this. Especially since it was kinda my fault. See, this is why I don't ask people for things. "Daddy, it's okay. I'm more concerned about you and this surgery."

"It's knee surgery, not brain surgery. I'll be alright. But your mother is gonna have to take some time off work to care for me so it's gonna be much tighter around here for awhile."

"Can't Omari get a job?" I asked, worried and afraid. My able-bodied, working age brother was upstairs, probably playing video games or something equally frivolous.

Mama shook her head. "There's no point. He's got a volunteer position and then football camp after that. It's fine. We'll be fine."

I looked at Daddy's face and knew that wasn't true at all.

2

I sat in my car in my parents' driveway, sweat pouring in rivers down my neck and back. All I could think about was how broken my daddy looked when he had to tell me no. The last time he said that word to me was when I was seventeen and begged him to let me get a tattoo. A tramp stamp, if I'm being real, and he was right to say no. But he hated doing it.

My daddy was raised at a time when men were expected to provide. Every moment he sat on that porch or in his recliner was another moment of him not working and, in his mind, being useless. And it wasn't even his fault.

And then there was my mother. Her mother, my Grandma Minty, had once gotten drunk on moonshine and let it slip to me that she and my granddaddy never wanted my mom to marry my dad. "He was a nice man but he didn't come from much," Minty said. "But your mother was lost in love. And that was the end of that." And now, all these years later, my mother sat on that back porch with my daddy, dreaming of the life she could have had.

That will never be me.

My mother raised me to have dreams and to

stop at nothing until I fulfilled them. And despite a few derailments of my own, I was close. So close. But I had to graduate first.

I wiped my forehead and stared at the clock on my cell. Only a few hours before I had to be at my shift at Port. Of all the things I saw myself doing at age 23, waitressing was not one of them. But the work was easy, the tips were pretty good, I ate there for free, and most important, the hours were flexible.

I clicked on my banking app to check my account, because my old pastor said if you name it and claim it, He will do it for you. I entered my password and closed my eyes. "I claim my thousand dollars. Right now!" I opened my eyes.

$12.39.

My half of the rent was $460. I was not gonna make that much in tips in one-and-a-half days. Shit. And my other job, mystery shopping, wouldn't have any more gigs until the end of the month.

My plan was to use $10 for gas and then whatever I got in tips tonight would go toward my credit card bill and my little bit of groceries for the week. I guess I could let the credit card payment be late. The worst they could do is harass me.

And then right at that moment, as if they knew what I was thinking, I got a text from petty-ass Verizon. "Your past-due balance of $128.71 is due immediately. Failure to clear this balance will result in service interruption."

FML.

I had one more ace up my sleeve. I've always

hate to play this card but I was desperate.

I took a deep breath and almost choked on the hot air. I scrolled down my contacts until I got to him. I pushed the call button. Lord help me.

"Aye gul!" Cal yelled into the phone. Caltron Middlebrooks. My ex. And no, that's not a typo. I can see why you would think his name was Carlton because that actually makes sense. But no, his actual name is Caltron. Cal-Tron. Don't ask me, I didn't pick it.

"Hey Cal. How are you?"

"Busy. What you want?"

How I'd missed his charm. "Damn, Cal. It's like that? How's the business going?"

He laughed. "Which one?"

He might be an asshole at times but I'll give him credit for one thing: Cal knows how to hustle. At 28, he owns a wing truck, a landscaping service, he's part owner of a beauty supply store, and he sells insurance. He's the logical choice for a loan. It's just...the cost is high. And by cost, I mean his expectations. And by his expectations, I mean me. And by me, I mean ass. And while sex with Cal is hardly the worst thing in the world, my heart wasn't in it anymore and we both knew it. The last time we met up, it just felt awkward.

"Alright, since you're so busy, I'll cut to the chase. I'm running short this month and I really need to borrow some money to make rent."

His long silence told me something was up.

"Hello?"

"Yeah, I'm here. You talked to your folks already?"

That was weird. Last time he asked how much and transferred to it my account immediately.

"Yeah, they're strapped. My dad is about to have knee surgery and things are pretty tight."

"You ain't got no other people?" he said, smacking into the phone. He was probably eating wings.

"You know I hate being a burden," I said.

"So what's wrong with living back home till you get on your feet?"

"There's no room for me. And you know there's still some...issues I haven't worked through yet. I wouldn't be comfortable there." He knew all about my issues. He'd been the one to nurse me through them.

Cal sighed and my heart sank. "Okay, here's where I'm at with it. You remember Kiana?"

Oh. Now it all made sense. "Yeah. How's she doing?"

"She good. The thing is, we're serious now and I don't think it would be fair to her for me to be giving my ex money. Especially if the ex is you."

"I see."

"Come on, girl, don't be like that. You know I would if I could. $460 ain't shit to me."

"Gee, thanks for saying that."

Cal chuckled. "My bad. I ain't mean it like that. I'm just saying, if it was just about me, it would be in your account right now. But I gotta think about her. You know what I mean?"

"I know what you mean." I was truly at a low point because I was willing to reduce myself to begging. "Even if I promised to pay you back? With interest?"

"Sorry, Mani."

I let out the breath I'd been holding and closed my eyes. "It's okay. See, this is why I don't like asking people for shit."

Cal was quiet for a moment before saying, "Take care of yourself, Mani. You gon' be alright."

The tears fell as I hung up and I prayed he was right.

3

You know how they say "when it rains, it pours"? It's never that simple for me. In my life, when it rains, it floods, and then lightning hits the generator so there's no power, and then a tornado comes through and destroys my house, and then I slip on a wet leaf and break my neck.

So I was at work, right? The day was going fine. Port is an upscale dive, if that's a thing, and it sits just north of downtown which I love because it's only a 10-minute drive from school. An added bonus? The clientele usually tips well.

Port attracts douchey frat boy types who work from downtown all the way up to Buckhead. I'd say about half of them are MBAs and the others are attorneys, medical professionals, sports industry professionals and other miscellaneous suit-wearing loud mouths looking to turn up before they venture out into Atlanta traffic.

Like I said, these types tip well for the most part but on very rare occasions, I get some country confederate flag waver in a suit in my section. And of course it happened to me today. Of *course*.

His name was Paul, and everything was all good

until he lied and said he ordered the double Port burger with no tomatoes and no Port sauce. I knew it was a lie and my boss, Fran, knew it, too. But the customer is always right, blah, blah, blah, so we remade the already half-eaten meal. Fine, it happens.

Then he insisted that his drink was too strong. Too strong. Who complains about that?

But I went to the bar and had them fix it. Here's where things went all the way left: he asked me if my hair was real. I'm used to that. I got my thick, jet black hair from my mother, and my twistouts have actually stopped traffic. But I've always wondered, deep down, if my brown skin made people think my hair was fake. It's rare that Farrah, my light-skinned Michael Jackson, gets comments like that.

Here's how it went.

"Say," he said through his ugly teeth, "that hair of yours. Is that real? Or is it like...synthetic?"

"It's my hair."

He laughed. "Yours as in grew out of your head or yours as in you 'bought it?'" he said, complete with air quotes.

I plastered on a smile. "It's growing out of my head, sir."

"Hey, hey. None of that sir stuff. I told you my name is Paul."

"Can I get you anything else, Paul?" I asked, itching to get away from his drunk ass.

"Eh, how about..." he trailed off and then things seemed to move in slow motion. Paul reached up and grabbed a handful of my hair, and then he proceeded to yank it. As you can imagine, that didn't go over well.

"Hey! What the fuck are you doing?" I asked as I struggled to get out of his grasp.

"Oh come on! You know you like hair pulling. Don't act all shy!"

He was right. I did like it, but not in that context and not when his grubby hands were doing it. As I struggled to loosen his grip, I felt something brush past me and before I knew it, I was free.

I stumbled backwards and fell to the floor as two men, one of them Paul, struggled a few feet away. I couldn't see the other guy well but he was obviously strong because he had Paul in a headlock inside of five seconds. As Paul struggled for his own freedom, Fran ran in from the back and helped me up.

"Oh my God!" she said, a horrified look on her face. "What did he do to you?"

I hadn't even realized I was crying. I was mostly dazed and confused. "He was yanking on my hair," I said, my voice cracking.

She held my arm while I steadied myself on my feet. "Okay, go on back and clean yourself up. I'll take care of that piece of shit."

I hurried to the restroom and closed and locked the door behind me. I looked in the mirror and was shocked at my reflection. No wonder Fran had looked so alarmed.

I hadn't even felt it, but at some point, Paul had scratched my face. A long, dark pink welt had already sprouted on my face and the sting it brought with it was getting more intense. My hair was every-where but that was easily fixed with a few swipes of my fingertips. I was blowing my nose when someone knocked on the door.

"Someone's in here!"

"It's me. Let me in."

I unlocked the door and Fran burst in. Her usu-ally neat red hair was out of place and she was breath-ing hard. She was somewhere in her 40s and still in good shape. I wondered if she had jumped into the fray. She was that type.

"Is he still out there?" I asked.

"No, he's locked in my office with Fernando. The police are on their way."

"Police?"

"He assaulted you, didn't he?"

I was barely thinking straight. "Well, yeah. I guess. I think he was trying to be funny and was too drunk to control himself."

"Don't make excuses for that prick. Here, let me put some peroxide on that. Lord only knows where his hands have been."

"I don't wanna deal with the police. Just tell them I'm not pressing charges."

"Why would I do that?"

"You know why."

Fran's face fell. She must have forgotten that I was still dealing with the fallout from an incident in my past. Without another word, she applied peroxide to my scratch with a cotton ball. It stung intensely at first, then faded into a dull burning. "Who was the guy who helped me?"

"I don't know. Your knight in shining armor, I suppose." She smiled and I smiled back. I hoped he was still out there. I wanted to buy him a drink.

We exited the bathroom and walked back to the front. I looked around for a minute before realizing I didn't know what this guy looked like. I only remembered a blue t-shirt and a black baseball cap. There was no one there fitting that description. Damn, I had wanted to thank him.

"Looking for me?" a voice said behind me.

I whirled around and there he was. Black guy, about 5'11, brown-skin, very nice smile. Like Laz Alonso if he was a few shades darker. His hat was pulled low and he was wearing sunglasses. I couldn't see his eyes. "I was, actually. I wanted to thank you for helping me a minute ago."

"You're welcome. It's what I do," he said with a smile. Kinda corny but okay.

"Can I get you a drink? On the house."

"That's okay. I don't drink at lunch."

"Then why are you in a bar?"

He frowned. "Did I miss the announcement that y'all don't serve food anymore?" The sarcasm was biting and I felt like an idiot. It really was a dumb question.

I ignored the jab. "Then do you want some fries? A burger? On the house, last chance."

He stared at me, or I think he did. Couldn't really tell behind the glasses and hat. "Okay. Gimme a Port, no bacon, and fries."

"Want a Shirley Temple with that?" I said.

The man laughed. "You got jokes? Okay, you know what? Just for that, I do want a Shirley Temple. And don't forget my damn cherry."

I giggled and made my way back to the kitchen with his order. I had just put it in when Fran grabbed my elbow. She ushered me over to a booth and I momentarily forgot about the knight.

"Are you okay?" she asked.

"I'm fine. I'll put some ointment on it when I get home. It's nothing."

"I don't mean that, I mean...you know. Being attacked again."

"Oh, that. I'm a little shook but I'll be okay.

"Well what about in general? You've been moping around here for days and I'm worried." Her face was creased with concern for me.

I patted her hand. "You're sweet but I'm good. Just money stuff. It's boring, trust me."

Without another word, Fran walked over to the bar. A minute later, she came back with two shots. "Let's do this."

Ah, yes. *This*. We'd done *this* many times. After the thing with my ex, Eric. After I broke up with Cal. After her husband divorced her for his dental hygienist. After my Grandma Minty died. And most recently, when her sixteen-year-old daughter Ariana got knocked up. We drank and she reached over and squeezed my hand, silently telling me it would be okay.

"How much money do you need?" she said.

I shook my head rapidly. "Stop."

"Imani,--"

"No. I can't. Please don't bring it up again."

"Fine."

We sat in silence and listened to the restaurant sounds around us. Forks scraped against plates, ice cubes rattled inside their glasses, and patrons' voices melded together in an indistinguishable hum.

"Okay, don't laugh at me," she said, "but I think I might have an answer to your financial problems."

"I'll try anything at this point."

"Britney sent me this article on sugar babies. Did you know there are more of them at your school than any other school in the country?"

"I would have no reason to know that."

"All I could think when I read it was 'Mani would be perfect for this.'"

I laughed. I couldn't help it. "Girl, bye."

"No. Girl, hi." We both burst out laughing. "No, I'm serious. I see the way these guys in here look at you. You're young and everything is still perky and you haven't had any kids stretching your hoo-ha all out to be damned. This is perfect."

"First of all, no. Second of all, how would I even start? I don't even--what, stand on the corner? Advertise on Instagram? No, Fran."

"There's a website. You join it, put up a profile, and the guys find you. Rich guys."

I smiled at the absurdity of it. "You're actually serious."

She shrugged. "What's the harm? You probably

don't even have to fuck these guys. Not all of them, anyway."

I giggled and felt my muscles relaxing from the shot. "You sure know how to take a girl's mind off her troubles, I'll give you that."

Fran shrugged and sat back against the booth. Her freckles and long hair made her look younger, but the red lipstick she wore every single day did not. The woman hated trends.

Just then, Sam signaled me from the kitchen. "Let me take this food to the knight. Take it out of my check."

"Ain't you broke enough already?" she asked.

I shot a bird at her and walked back and grabbed the plates. When I got to the knight's table, he already had his drink. "Here you go, sir. I see you have your Shirley Temple already. You're gonna want to drink that slowly. Are you driving?"

He laughed. "That's funny. Thanks for this."

"It's the least I could do. I appreciate it."

"You needed help. I couldn't go out like that. What kind of man would I be if I didn't step in?"

True. I watched him bite into his burger and was at a loss for a witty response. I could tell he was cute under that hat, and his back muscles were visible through his t-shirt. I stopped myself from staring. "Believe it or not, most wouldn't have done what you did. So thank you. Take care."

"You too," he said as I walked away.

4

"Here, bitch. Take this money."

Farrah snatched the cash from my hand. "Thanks, hoe."

I did it. I used my school money for my rent. I had no other choice, y'all. I couldn't go back to my parents' house. Not in a million, trillion years. But I would be fine. My school money was a safety net but it was really just a product of my own paranoia. Financial aid always came through. It had been late a few times, but I was always able to get back in my classes after being dropped. My school fund was my way of making sure everything went smoothly. It wasn't nearly enough to cover full tuition but it was enough to put a deposit on a payment plan. But I didn't foresee it being necessary.

Farrah handed me her laptop and plopped onto the couch next to me. "I am so bored with life right now."

"Yes, it must be so boring to have a good job and lots of friends and a nice car. You're in my prayers."

She laughed and poked me with her big toe, which was painted the perfect shade of pink. "I need a boyfriend."

I glared at her over the laptop screen. "What the hell for?"

"I don't know, actually. I'm not trying to get married for another five years or so. If I even decide to get married. I don't know about cuffing niggas these days. They're all so feminine now. Wanting you to wine and dine them and shit. I refuse."

I pulled up my school's website and typed in my username and password, barely listening, letting out an occasional, "mm hm."

If I wanted to graduate in the spring, I had to go full-time. It was gonna be tough with work but I knew I could do it if I really buckled down and worked my ass off. I was grateful not to have a boyfriend at this point. Men are unnecessary distractions. Always.

Look at my mother. I love my daddy, Lord knows I do, but my mother waits on him hand and foot now. I know marriage is in sickness and in health but her primary focus is him, and it's hard to watch sometimes. And I have yet, in all my 23 years, to see the reverse in action.

There, I was logged in. I went to the registration screen and my heart pounded in excitement when I read my classification. I was officially a senior! And that meant all my classes would be in my major.

My dream is to sell luxury homes. And while I don't *have* to get a degree to do this, I need a degree to do it right and to stop the generational curse in my family of wanting something and not knowing or having the tools I need to get it. That ends with me.

At the end of my ten-year plan, I saw myself

owning my own luxury real estate firm with at least twenty employees working under me. I didn't have it all worked out yet but I had the basic blueprint. My vision board was full of big beautiful homes, a few stylish offices, and lots of cash. There was no man on there, yet, but I had plenty of time for that. For now, there was only school.

I clicked here and clicked there, registering for every class I needed and getting in all of them thanks to my status as a senior and a tier one registrant.

"...so I figure if I do decide to have kids, my mother will expect me to have a husband, too. Girl, I guess," Farrah was saying.

"Mm hm," I hummed absentmindedly. And then I saw it. "No, no, no, no!" I said.

Farrah sat up and leaned over to see the screen. "What's wrong?"

I pointed, too stunned to speak.

Farrah read the words aloud, although it was totally unnecessary. They were seared into my brain. "You are ineligible for federal aid. What? Why?"

I had no answers for her, or for myself. All I had were hot, salty tears.

As it turns out, Farrah explained after logging on and checking my FAFSA for me, I had already received the most aid they were gonna give me. And while it's true that it's taken me much longer to finish school than I had hoped, and I had used some of my refund money for bills and maybe a little foolishness, I never thought this would happen. I just assumed the feds were an endless fount of student loan money. Why wouldn't they be, as long as you promised to repay?

Well now we know. It doesn't work like that.

I waited for exactly 83 agonizing minutes before someone named Tammy in the financial aid office finally took me off of hold. She confirmed what I already knew, and what was the absolute worst news I could have gotten: There was nothing she, or the school, could do. Yes, this happens all the time. No, they won't increase the limit. Yes, she was sure. You're welcome, and have a good day.

I was inconsolable, so Farrah finally left me alone in my room. I had just enough money left in my account to cover student fees. Which meant I could go to the campus and work out in the gym if I wanted, but taking an actual class? Out of my reach now.

Fuck!

I cried some more and weighed my options. Classes were to start in 48 days. At the end of the first week, they deregister anyone who hasn't paid. I thought about the person who hits that button and imagined him or her to be like the Wizard of Oz, hidden in a booth behind a curtain making unilateral decisions about other peoples' lives. The Great Deregistrator.

Anyway, I calculated that I had about 55 days to get my shit together. What to do? What to do? My credit cards were maxed out and no bank in its right mind would lend me a dime. If I worked a shift at Port's every night and mystery shopped every morning and afternoon and got a part-time job working a third shift, I could probably earn enough to pay half of my tuition.

I picked up the phone to call my daddy. Not for money. Just for some encouragement. No matter what happened, he always had just the right words to lift her spirits. But when I went to speed dial and pressed my daddy's picture, it rang once and then petty-ass Verizon lady jumped in. "I'm sorry, your account has been--"

I slammed the phone down and screamed in frustration. Farrah burst through my door. "What now?" she asked, her eyes wide.

I sat there and took a few deep breaths, trying to be rational. And then I asked myself the question I always asked when I didn't know how to handle something. What would Beyoncé do?

"Farrah, let me use your cell phone real quick. I need to call Fran."

5

If you thought I was calling Fran for a loan, you were close. I was calling her about money but I didn't want it from her. I wanted to get it for myself. I just needed that article she read.

Four read-throughs of the article entitled "Life in the Sugar Bowl" and a lot of googling later, Farrah and I set up my profile on Top Shelf. I apologized to Beyoncé in my head because I was pretty damn sure she would never do *this*. But I couldn't think about that now. I had a goal and 55 days to make it. The Deregistrator wasn't getting me this time.

The process of setting up a profile was annoying. The personal questions alone were over the line-- why did they need to know my lingerie size?--but those were just the appetizer. The main course was the documents they required. One form of government ID, a scan of your last STI panel, proof of enrollment for student applicants, four pictures, each from a different angle, and your most recent playlist. The last one was hella random but whatever.

Luckily, I got a full STI panel done after me and Cal broke up. I'm not proud of this but we stopped using protection about three months in. If I told you about the sex, you'd understand why but that's another story. Maybe I'll tell you. Just not right now. But he's why I had that on hand, and it was a good thing I did because I needed this process to go as quickly as possible.

I leaned back against the couch pillows. "It's probably too late to worry about this now," I said, "but my family can never find out about this. My dad, especially. He would be so disappointed. And my little brothers, oh my God."

Farrah ate a strawberries and cream popsicle and contemplated that for a moment. She was always eating, with her greedy ass. And she still stayed a size 4 no matter what. Tiny bitch. "As long as your dad and brothers aren't looking to sponsor young women, I think you'll be okay."

"Yeah. You're right. That makes sense."

She peered at the screen. "Okay, it's asking for a credit report."

"What?" I looked where her finger was pointing. "Girl, that's for the sugar daddies. You almost gave me a heart attack."

"Sorry." Farrah tapped her fingers on her desk. "Is your credit that bad?"

She knew a little of my finances but I kept the most embarrassing aspects to myself. 598 is not a pretty number. "It's not where I want it to be."

Farrah didn't respond to that. "I should join, too."

"Why would *you* join? You're not short on cash."

"I know, but I'm so booooored."

I had to laugh. "Get a life."

"I'm trying!"

"You don't have to do this, Farrah."

"Whatever, Drake. I'm doing it."

And that's how Farrah and I came to sugar babies. I'll be honest: we're both very attractive but I think she's prettier and she thinks I'm prettier. Maybe deep down, we're both shallow, conceited, pretty bitches who say what we think the other wants to hear. Nobody's truly objective about their own looks, right?

I studied my best friend and wondered why on earth she wanted to do this. I'm sure working 9 to 5 as a junior loan officer isn't the most thrilling job in the world but she had a steady paycheck and she was working in her field. That's a lot more than I could say for myself. And I don't know, maybe I'm a little jealous of her. The Coopers aren't rich or anything but they're stable and comfortable.

I would have given anything to be stable and comfortable instead of moving from apartment to apartment, school to school, having to make new friends and avoid new enemies. Not being able to answer the phone in case it was a creditor calling and, at one point, having to live in that disgusting extended stay motel. I love my parents but their troubles affected me in ways I don't like to think about. And in ways Farrah has never had to think about.

So why was she so eager to do...this? Then again, why was *I*? I'm not the most devout person but I do believe in God and I try to live by the Bible passages I read when I was younger and attending church faith-fully. Could I even call myself a good person after using men for money? On purpose?

I guess we'll see.

At any rate, Farrah and I were both approved by the next afternoon. All that was left to do was wait for some rich, handsome man to reach out to us. We were ready. And I had exactly 54 days before my day of reckoning. It was on.

6

So you know all those rich, handsome men who were waiting eagerly in front of their computers for a chance to contact us? Yeah, they don't exist. To be clear, there are lots of rich men. There are also a good number of handsome men. The bad news is that, from what I can see, these attributes rarely exist in the same package.

FML.

Jay Z said there's no such thing as an ugly billionaire. I have no experience with that so I'll take his word for it. But millionaires? Chile...

But let me back up. On day 53 of my countdown, I hunkered down in my bedroom with a Bojangles chicken biscuit and a glass of sweet tea and really researched this whole sugar baby thing. I needed to know what I was getting into and I didn't have anyone to talk to about it. And wouldn't you know, there are whole online message boards devoted to the lifestyle. You can literally find anything on Al Gore's internet. Wow.

I joined Candy Girls, an online forum for girls in the sugar bowl, as they call it. It was just one of several such websites but CG seemed more college-girl friendly. It had several subforums, one for each sugaring website. I joined subforum for Top Shelf and chose BadGradgirl as my username which...I know, it sounds corny, but I was in a hurry. I had a shift tonight so I only had a few hours to learn this stuff.

I don't know where I got this from but I had gone into this with the impression that the extent of sugaring was looking pretty and asking for money at the end of the date. I was already good at the former and I figured I could learn to be great at the latter. But the reality of it appeared to be quite different. And as I read the FAQs and tips and pointers, I began to feel a growing sense of uneasiness, like I was in way over my head.

I was also disappointed. So many of the girls on the forum said to stay away from black men. They even call them Splenda daddies. Okay, that's kind of funny if I'm being honest, but still. I prefer black men. Their skin, their hair, their swagger, their power. I was made for them and they were made for me. Nobody else does it for me. Period.

However...this wasn't about love. I had the rest of my life to marry a black man. This was about cash.

Speaking of cash, I discovered that, just as it was with Cal, the cost of all this free money is high. Apparently, platonic sugar daddies don't truly exist. So all hopes I had of getting paid for the mere pleasure of my company were dashed.

Could I really do this?

Mrs. Araminta Gill-Reese, my beloved Grandma Minty who I miss dearly, once told me a wet ass and a dry purse don't match. If I twisted it a little, I could almost rationalize that she would have seen nothing wrong with what I planned to do. She may have even encouraged it.

And let's just be real. We've all slept with folks for free, often the wrong person, and come away with nothing but a heart full of shame and regret. Adding money to that equation didn't make the situation any worse. Right?

Once I convinced myself that was true, I felt a little bit better about moving forward. And then I was surprised to see I had gotten my first private message.

His name was William but he went by Bill. He didn't say much in his message other than that he would like to correspond to determine whether we might be compatible. He urged me to look at his profile to see if I was interested. I took a last bite of biscuit and, after taking a deep breath, clicked his profile.

Here we go.

Bill wasn't handsome. I guess I'd describe him as average but well-preserved, and by this point, I was okay with that. I couldn't afford to be picky with only 53 days left. I'd scrolled through enough profiles to see that my expectations had been too high. The important thing was that he wasn't ugly, and for me, Bill's averageness was a win.

He was white, with smooth tanned skin and salt and pepper hair. He was in his late 40s with adult children and two ex-wives. Bill said he wasn't looking for love, he was looking for companionship. That whole not looking for love thing was certainly in line with my own feelings on the matter, so I counted it as another win. And finally, Bill was a hedge fund manager. I wasn't sure what that meant, but I'd heard the term enough that I understood the context clues. Bill had money.

I took a sip of sweet tea and clicked "yes."

Here's something else I learned about Bill: he must have been sitting at his computer waiting for a response because I wasn't even done with my tea when he messaged me back. I was nervous, but also elated. It was day 53 and I was feeling ahead of the game.

This will be easy.

All that confidence I had waned on day 50 of my countdown. The day I was to meet Bill.

He suggested we meet for coffee. Many of the candy girls suggested letting him pick the place, so I did, and I was relieved that he suggested You're Grounded, a cute little coffee bar in downtown Decatur. I knew the area well so I wouldn't feel completely out of my element.

About three hours before our...appointment? It wasn't a date, was it? I wasn't sure, so I'll call it an appointment. Anyway, I thought, and thought, and obsessed about what to wear. I didn't wanna look cheap, and by cheap, I don't mean slutty. I mean literally cheap. Most of my sartorial choices hinged on whether or not Forever 21 or Kohl's was having a sale.

"What's the vibe you're going for?" Farrah asked from inside my tiny closet. "Cute? Girl next door? Fun? Flirty? Educated thot? Give me something, Mani."

I was sitting on my bed lotioning my legs and trying not to freak out. "I don't know. Cute and un-bothered. Maybe a maxi dress?"

"Too bohemian."

"Jeans and a shirt?"

"Too casual."

With my legs sufficiently moisturized, I turned my attention to my face. Black don't crack but you still have to care for the foundation. "T-shirt dress?"

"Hmm. That could work. Grey or black?"

"Grey."

We paired it with my nude gladiator sandals and a tan crossbody bag. It wasn't something I'd ever thought about before, but suddenly, I was self-conscious about the lack of designer label. Perhaps Bill wouldn't notice.

Farrah did my makeup--a light beat with bronzer and nude lip-gloss. Perfect look for a summer afternoon. We piled my hair up into a curly puff and she gelled down my baby hairs. Would Bill even appreciate baby hairs? I'd see shortly.

"You look beautiful," Farrah said. "How are you feeling?"

"I'm nervous. Look at my hand," I said, holding it out so she could see the shaking. "Help me calm down."

"You want some weed?"

I rolled my eyes. "Yes. That's exactly what I need. There's nothing sexier than showing up to a first date smelling like dank."

Farrah laughed and grabbed her chicken wings off the dresser. "Not a date. Appointment."

"Whatever. Trade places with me?"

"If I do I'm keeping the money."

I smiled but didn't laugh. Farrah poked her lower lip out. "Aww. It's okay. You'll be fine. I have all his info and I know where you're going and our phones are linked."

"Yeah but my phone is off," I reminded her.

"You should still be able to get internet. Just make sure you hook up to the Wi-Fi as soon as you get there."

I nodded and took a deep breath.

"And here," she said, handing me her keys. "Take my car so your makeup doesn't run."

The cold, clanging metal felt good as it dropped into my hand. "Have I told you how much I love you?"

Farrah winked and smiled at me. "Go get him, girl."

7

Bill was sitting at the table closest to the back door just like he'd said in his message. He had joked that he chose that spot "so you can have an easy exit if you think I'm a creep." I know he was joking but I hate that he said it because it was already in my head. That just made it worse.

Nevertheless, I approached Bill the Hedge Fund Manager and Possible Creep with a big smile on my face. He rose when he saw me and I noticed how well put together he looked. He wasn't dressed up; rather, he wore a pink button down shirt, freshly starched, and light blue chino shorts. Boat shoes completed the look, and honestly, he looked like money.

He looked a tad bit better than his picture, and I was genuinely happy about that. He kissed my left cheek and held my chair out, pushing it toward the table after I sat.

"It's lovely to meet you, Imani."

"You too, Bill. You did say you prefer Bill, right?"

"Right." He looked at me with piercing green eyes. "Should we go ahead and address the elephant in the room?"

Uh oh. "What's that?"

"I'm your first, right?"

"Oh," I said with a giggle, a little relieved and a little embarrassed. No sense lying about it. "What gave me away?"

"Well for one, you're nervous, which I find really cute, by the way. But also, it's the way you're dressed."

I kept my smile plastered on but inside, I was weeping over my terrible fashions. "Is something wrong?"

"No, no, no, you look beautiful. You look perfect, actually. I'm just used to women being supremely overdressed."

Thank goodness. "Well, it *is* Atlanta."

"That's very true," he said with a laugh. This wasn't unpleasant, and he actually looked kinda good when he smiled. I started to relax a little. I even managed to remember some of the tips I'd read on Candy Girls.

"So Bill, I've actually never been here before. What do you suggest?" I asked, relying on his expertise.

"I like the French press, myself."

Shit. What the hell is a French press? And it's not like I could quickly google it because I had forgotten to get on the Wi-Fi. Damn, damn, damn. "Okay, I'll have that."

Bill chuckled again and I wondered if he was laughing at me. I'm not a bama, y'all, I swear. It's just...my world is somewhat small. I've only left the country once, and that was for a beach vacay in Jamaica. It was the best trip I've ever been on but Bill would probably laugh at that, too. And it wasn't that he was white, or rich. His whole aura screamed worldly, and I'm just a regular Georgia peach.

I logged onto the Wi-Fi while he was getting our French presses, then I took the moment to look around me. Lots of families. A few students on their laptops. Several adult professionals on phones or having meetings. It was just a normal day. Everything about this was perfectly normal.

Bill returned and placed a baby blue mug in front of me. The steam wafted into my nostrils and the strong aroma made my eyes water. I had forgotten an important fact: I don't drink coffee. And if I was ever gonna start, I would ease into it with, like, Folgers or something. This was uncharted territory, and I prayed I wouldn't get bubble guts.

"So Bill," I said, taking some control like the girls recommended, "tell me a little about yourself. Your profile said you're a hedge fund manager."

"Yeah, but I'm afraid it's not all that interesting. A lot of numbers and such." He took a sip and didn't blink at the heat. "Do you by any chance invest in the stock market?"

"Actually yes. I opened a Sharebuilder account when I was 18. I had no idea what I was doing but I bought a few shares of Disney, IBM, and a few others. Back then they would say 'buy stocks in companies you patronize.'"

He smiled. "They still say that. Well good, that's very good. Smart to get in when you're young."

I nodded. I'd sold that stock years ago to pay for a trip to Vegas to celebrate Farrah's birthday but he didn't need to know that. "What made you want to be a hedge fund manager?"

"Money," he answered immediately. "I could conjure up some altruistic reason but it would be bullshit. I like money."

"That's a perfectly good reason to do what you do. To do any job, really," I said. "And now that you have money, you can do all the altruistic stuff you want. From your yacht."

That got a big laugh out of him. "So tell me about you. Your profile said you're a college student."

"I am. I'm in my last year. Nontraditional student. I kinda took a few detours on the road to my degree but I'm almost there. Real Estate."

"Nice. Are you a first-generation college student?"

Hmm. That one pinged my radar a bit. "Yes. Why do you ask?"

Bill shrugged. "I've heard it said that first-generation students are less likely to finish in four years. And that makes perfect sense to me because there really isn't a roadmap, right?"

"Right," I said cautiously.

"But when you have children, you'll have that roadmap so their paths will be clearer than yours was."

It made sense, and I was relieved that the conversation hadn't gone where I thought it was going.

"Why Real Estate?" he asked.

"It's just always been my dream to sell luxury homes."

Bill's eyebrows shot up. "Well now you have a connection. My friends are constantly buying and selling real estate."

I nodded. "Sounds good."

"What's wrong?" he asked.

I couldn't believe he picked up on my discomfort. I briefly debated with myself before blurting it out. "Would they buy and sell with *me*, though?"

He sighed and nodded. "That's actually a good question. I want to say of course they would but I suppose that's easy for me to say since I've never had anyone not deal with me before. Sorry."

"Oh, no! Don't be sorry at all! I think it's amazing that you see it from my perspective." The girls said to never let him have a negative thought when he's in your presence. "You strike me as a progressive guy." I think that smoothed it over.

Yep, there it was. A smile. "So listen," he said. "I'm interested. I'd like to know where you want to go from here."

Here we go.

The girls said this would happen. He just made me an offer, and now he was expecting me to negotiate. But I've always struggled with that. How do you determine your own worth? And I don't mean in that annoying, meme-ish, "add tax to it" bullshit kind of way. I mean truly, how do you determine what your particular skills, or time, or love are worth?

My French press sat untouched but Bill didn't

seem to notice. "I wouldn't mind getting together again. My classes don't start for another month or so. Now would be the time to get to know me, if you're so inclined."

"I'm inclined," he said, his eyes never leaving my lips. I briefly wondered what sex might be like with him. "Why don't we do lunch next time," he continued. "You can pick the place."

I tried to work up the nerve to talk money but I just couldn't. I was afraid to scare him off.

I was also hoping I wouldn't have to bring this up but now I had to. The words didn't want to leave my mouth but I forced them to. "I'll be honest with you. I don't have phone service at the moment so if you wanted to get in contact with me, that might pose a problem."

Goodness, I sounded like such a basic bitch.

Bill didn't bat an eye, though. "Well that's no good. I'll need to call you to finalize our lunch plans. Who do you have?"

"Verizon."

He rolled his eyes and pulled out his wallet. "I hope this will cover that," he said as he slid a one-hundred-dollar bill toward me. It wouldn't, but I now had more money than I did when I left my apartment. It was a good start. If I had more experience, I would have gone for more but I didn't have my footing yet. I played it safe.

The girls said not to look too eager or excited so I simply smiled and thanked him. "I suppose we should exchange numbers now," I said.

He passed me his phone and I put in my contact info. I passed it back and picked up my own. "Number?"

He gave me his number and we finished our appointment. All I could think of was that I needed to pay that damn cell bill. What if he called and it was still disconnected? Shit. I was still $28 short.

It's always something!

8

I rushed home from my date with Bill. I wouldn't say I was on cloud 9 or anything but he had certainly made an impression and I couldn't wait to tell Farrah. She was on the couch waiting when I came through the door.

"Why the hell didn't you message me? I was so worried! I was about to drive up there but then I got outside and remembered you had my car. What the hell?"

"I know, I know, I'm sorry. I got so flustered I forgot to get on the Wi-Fi when I got there. But I'm fine, see?" I said, whirling around so she could see that I was still in one piece.

"Okay. I'm glad you're okay," she said more calmly. "So how was it?"

I smiled involuntarily and sat next to her. "It went really well, actually. I was surprised. He looked better than his picture and he was really nice. He kinda sniffed me out though. He knew it was my first time."

"Was that the first white guy you've been out with?"

"Not the first, but definitely the best. And he

gave me this," I said as I pulled Mr. Benjamin from my wallet.

"So you got $100 without any physical stuff?"

I nodded.

"Okay, I'm definitely doing this," she said, and we laughed together.

"It won't always be like this, though," I said with a mother's tone. "You need to read that forum. There are certain expectations and things you need to be aware of."

"I know, I know," she said.

"I'm serious, Farrah."

"I got it."

We sat in silence for a moment. I kicked my shoes off. "Okay, so I have one problem. He said he wants to text me and I told him about my phone issues. He gave me that money but I was too scared to ask for more. And now I still don't have enough to turn my phone back on. What do I do?"

Farrah rolled her eyes so far I thought they'd get stuck. "If you won't let me help you, the only other option is for you to transfer some of your school money."

"No," I said, shaking my head rapidly. "I can't."

"Why not?"

"I just can't."

"You're gonna earn it back anyway. What are you so afraid of?"

"You *know* what. If I don't finish--"

"You're gonna finish, Mani. But you have to have a little faith in yourself. You can't plan for everything.

You can't control every outcome. You just have to understand that. Look at this as an investment, not a failure."

I looked at my best friend and sighed. Everything was so simple in her world. Safety nets have that effect. But it's different for people like me, and that's something she would never understand.

I transferred the money from my school account and paid my cellphone bill begrudgingly. I told myself Farrah was right. It was an investment. And then I logged back in to The Top Shelf, wondering if I had any other messages. To my shock, there were 13!

My heart pounded and I felt a tingle of excitement. Thirteen men wanted to give me money. Now all I had to do is sift through them, which actually ended up being the fun part. It was like online shopping with a coupon for 100% off.

Ten of them were white, two were Asian, and one was black. With the Candy Girls' words in the back of my mind--Cheap! Splenda daddies!--I clicked the black guy's message first. His name was Shawn, and he simply said,

Hello, Imani. Your picture is worth 1,000 words and all of them are YES.

Oh, word? That's what we're doing?

I was intrigued. I clicked his profile to see what else he was working with besides good game. MBA, manager at a real estate firm, no kids, never been married, and he was looking for companionship and experiences. I knew what that meant.

Still, I was still feeling that tingle of excitement at his message and his picture intrigued me. It was just his eye--some guys refused to show their whole face. That sucked because you never know what you're gonna get but it made sense because money was supposed to be the big draw anyway. But his eye was kinda cute and I liked the way he came at me. I've always been a sucker for stimulating conversation, wordplay, and a sexy give-and-take. Sort of like the Knight.

The Knight. I wondered what made him pop into my head.

At any rate, I sat there for ten minutes obsessing over what I would say in my message back to Shawn. Finally, I settled on this:

> *Hi Shawn. Send me another message and see*
> *if you can turn my maybe into a yes.*

Not my finest work, but it would do.

Shawn wasn't like Bill. It wasn't until I got home from my shift at Port that he messaged me back. A seven-hour turnaround versus sixty seconds. I told myself to stop comparing. This wasn't about love or courtship. This was business. Anyway, he said,

> *The button is right there at the top right corner of*
> *your screen, sweetheart. We both know you want to*
> *click yes so just do it. You won't be disappointed.*

A smile crept across my lips as I clicked YES. Day 50 was shaping up quite nicely.

We met two days later, on day 48 of my countdown. I had a mild panic attack while standing in my closet because Shawn suggested the Bamboo Lounge and I most certainly could not wear a t-shirt dress to that spot. Farrah wasn't there to help me this time so I forced myself to relax. I was the one in control. *He* wanted *me*, not the other way around. Besides, I still had Bill on the hook. Shawn was just icing.

Speaking of Bill, he texted me this morning, just to let me know he was thinking about me. I texted back that he was sweet and suggested that we carve out some time to discuss the next stage. The girls said not to meet him again until an arrangement was made. I hadn't yet decided how much I would ask for, and apparently the rates are based on where you live. Since Bill and I weren't meeting for another three days, those decisions could wait.

I finally decided on an outfit. You can't go wrong with a little black dress, so I donned my favorite. It was a slinky, one-shoulder number with just the right fit--tight enough to show my silhouette but not tight enough that you could make out my internal organs.

Like all my clothes, my favorite little black dress was cheap. More specifically, it was made of cheap poly blend and rayon. My shoes weren't much better; black stiletto sandals that tied at the ankle, also cheap, made of man-made something or other. My handbag was black and sparkly. I think I got it from TJ Maxx. It had no label and didn't really have style, either. As soon as I started making some real money, I was gonna invest in some nice pieces.

I had to drive my own car this time so I doubled

up on the deodorant and didn't wear any foundation. All in all, I wasn't feeling my best and I didn't think I looked my best. But I just kept reminding myself that Bill was my main guy. Shawn was just icing.

He told me to meet him at the bar and when I walked in, there were four different black guys at the bar and they all had their backs turned. I was mildly irritated that Shawn wasn't turned around so that I could find him and he could see me make an entrance. Was I supposed to tap each guy on the shoulder until I found him?

Not a good start, Shawn.

"Hi there, is it just you?" asked the cute blonde hostess.

"No, I'm meeting someone. It's kind of a blind date."

She smiled knowingly. "Gotcha. Did you wanna look around, or...?"

I sighed and thought for a second. "No, I'll just text him."

I pulled my phone out and just as I started typing, I heard a deep voice coming from my left side. "Imani?" it asked.

I turned my head and there he was. Smooth brown skin, jet black hair with a mustache and goatee to match, full lips I wanted to kiss immediately, and a gray suit that hung impeccably from his muscular frame. He smiled and it seemed familiar, but more important than that, I felt the tingle again. I knew instantly that this day, day 48, was going to be very different from day 50 and Bill.

I'm in trouble.

9

The hostess led us to our seats and Shawn was a gentleman, pulling out my chair and the whole nine. I was annoyed with myself for being nervous again. I had just done this two days ago. I should be a pro by now, or at least have the ability to be cool. But I wasn't cool. Shawn had me running hot.

"Is this okay, or do you want a different spot?" he asked, gesturing toward the other side of the room farthest from the kitchen.

"No, this is fine," I managed to get out. I think I sounded normal. I think.

"Good. It's nice to meet you. As impressed as I was by your pictures, I have to say, they didn't do you justice."

I smiled coquettishly and tilted my head slightly to the side. "Thank you, that's so sweet." I wanted to return the compliment but I didn't want to give away my real feelings before any money changed hands. This wasn't a date. I repeated that in my head several times. *This is not a date.*

If only my nether regions were on the same page.

Our waiter came and took our drink orders. I

asked for a Cosmo and the second the word left my mouth, I felt like a complete idiot. That's practically the official beverage of Basic Bitches. But if Shawn felt a way about it, he didn't let on. He ordered a Scotch.

"So Imani, why don't you tell me a little about yourself."

"I'm 23 years old. I'm working on my bachelor's in Real Estate. I'm actually going into my last year."

Unlike Bill, Shawn didn't even bat an eye at that.

"What about you?" I asked, unable to take my eyes off of his lips. They were so juicy.

"I have an MBA from Carnegie Mellon. I'm 37. And I think this may be of interest to you...I'm a managing partner of a real estate investment group."

I already knew that but I widened my eyes to indicate surprise. The girls said a lot of these guys like to mentor their companions in business so this had the potential to be huge. "That's quite a coincidence."

He flashed that smile again. "We're headquartered here in Atlanta but we have holdings all over the southeast. We're looking into expansion right now so that keeps me pretty busy."

"That sounds really interesting. Maybe I can pick your brain some time."

He spread his hands. "I'm ready whenever you are."

I'll admit it. I was turned on. All the way on. This was not good. I needed to get my mind right. Think clearly. But when our drinks arrived, I immediately took two large gulps. I told myself to slow down because Drunk Imani is a horny nutcase, but hell, the drink was tasty.

I decided I needed to take control sooner rather than later. "So I think we should get something out of the way."

"Oh yeah? What's that?" he asked as he leaned closer to me. The smell of his cologne hit me and it smelled delicious. I wanted to lick him.

"I think we should work out our arrangement now before this goes any further."

"Arrangement?" he asked, his eyebrows furrowed quizzically.

Hmm. That was weird.

I took a sip. "Right. I think I'd prefer pay-per-meet over an allowance, at least until we know each other better."

Shawn sat back in his seat and looked at me with a strange expression. It almost looked like...surprise. And then I began to wonder if I was dealing with a Splenda Daddy. Wouldn't that be just my luck?

Finally, he spoke. "Pay-per-meet sounds good to me. How much did you have in mind?"

Ugh, this part. "During the getting-to-know-each other phase, I think I'd be comfortable with $200 per meet. After that, we can talk about something more permanent." I took another sip. "If you're interested."

"Oh, I'm interested," he said, and my heart skipped a beat. "We can do that."

Internally, I breathed a huge sigh of relief. With that out of the way, I could finally relax a little bit.

I downed the rest of my drink. Shawn watched me curiously, and I began to wonder if I was doing something wrong.

We ordered our food--he got chicken teriyaki and I got a few sushi rolls. Then he ordered me a second Cosmo. He didn't seem embarrassed having to say it so I stopped being embarrassed to drink it. By the time I was halfway through it, I was feeling loose. Feeling good.

"Do you know how to use chopsticks?" he asked me after the waiter brought our utensils.

"You think I was about to sit here and eat sushi with my fork?" I asked playfully.

"Hey, you never know. I've seen it happen on a few dates."

"Maybe you should stop dating birds, then."

He laughed and took a sip of his scotch, his eyes never leaving my face. "Maybe you're right."

"Why never married?"

"Yeah, my folks ask me that all the time. I don't know. Just never met the right one, I guess."

"Then it's a good thing you met me."

"Yes it is." He glanced at my chest and didn't seem to care that I saw him. "I don't wanna seem too forward but how would you feel about coming to an event with me tomorrow?"

Well damn.

"What kind of event?" That information was vital because I didn't have shit in my closet that would do for a place fancier than this.

"It's a fundraiser. I'm on the board of this charity

and we have a dinner every year."

Be cool. "Is it formal?"

"Yes. Why, is that a problem?"

My guard was down and I was comfortable enough to tell him the truth. "I'll be honest. I'm a college girl so my wardrobe is mostly casual."

Shawn seemed to be thinking about it. "Well we can change that," he said.

"What do you mean?"

He smiled. That million-dollar smile. "Just eat your food. Leave that to me."

Well okay, then.

I didn't trust him enough to ride in his car yet so he told me to meet him at Phipps Plaza, which was about fifteen minutes north. He had valeted and I had parked my hotbox one street over so I still didn't know what he drove. I imagined something modest. After all, I read that book too, the one about the millionaire down the street. I bet he drove a Lexus or maybe even a Toyota. Something nice but not too flashy.

I sweated my way to Phipps and daydreamed about what we'd do when we arrived. My best guess was that he would give me my $200 and help me pick out a dress to buy so that I wouldn't embarrass him tomorrow. Although he was the almost 40-year-old showing up with someone young enough to be his daughter, so the embarrassment might be on his end, not mine.

I arrived and parked in the back of the lot at the

front entrance. I dabbed my face with blotting paper and touched up my lip-gloss before I exited my car. As I walked toward the door, I heard a voice behind me. "Walk that walk, girl," it said, and I whirled around and saw Shawn. He was leaning against the hood of a cream colored Porsche. I'm not a car person so I can't tell you the model or the year, but I can tell you that thing was fucking *beautiful.*

I smiled and waited for him to catch up, trying hard not to stare at that car. "You beat me here," I said.

"I tend to speed." He paused. "When I drive. Otherwise, I take my time."

I said nothing, but my body responded.

We entered the mall and it felt like the most natural thing in the world. We didn't know each other yet but this was easy. I'd been on dates where every moment was labored and plodding but this was comfortable. That scared me a bit, because this was not a date. Not at all. This was work.

We entered Saks and I tried to act like I'd been there before. It was a little overwhelming with all the mannequins and sales girls wearing much better clothes than I was. I wondered if anyone could look at us and tell what we were.

Shawn took me to the men's department and I thought that was odd. He approached the young black guy at the counter and spoke with him. They gestured at me a few times and I strained to hear what they were talking about. I finally sat in a leather chair as my heart raced. These were uncharted waters.

Shawn walked back over to me with the other

man in tow. "Imani, this is Milan. Me and Milan go way back. He's gonna help us pick out a dress for you."

I stood and shook Milan's hand. "Nice to meet you."

Milan nodded once. "Same. So what's the occasion?"

"The Safe Cell Gala," Shawn said.

"Oh, of course. Say no more. Let me grab Tiff and see what we can find."

Shawn sat next to me and touched my arm. "You good?"

"Yeah. Just a little overwhelmed."

"No need for that. It's a Gala we throw every year to raise money for Sickle Cell research."

"My cousin has it," I said.

He nodded. "My sister. She's been sick all her life."

"I'm sorry to hear that."

Shawn looked at the floor. "Yeah. My parents tried everything. She would get better for a minute and then something would happen and she'd right be back in the hospital."

"I'm sure that was hard for your family."

"It was. It still is, really." He cleared his throat and squeezed my arm. "But let's not talk about that. It's about you right now. What kind of gown do you usually go for?"

"Umm--"

"When's the last time you went to a formal event?"

Lordt. I started giggling and decided to be honest. "Prom."

Shawn roared with laughter and it felt good to make him happy after hearing about his sister. "I'm sorry, I'm not laughing at you. You're just..." he looked me up and down. "You're cute."

It was an endearing thing to say to a woman you've known for three hours. I didn't know how to respond so I simply smiled and tapped the back of his hand with my fingers. It was my first time touching him voluntarily, and I could swear there was energy in that touch. Electricity. We stared into each other's eyes for a moment and I was afraid to stand up. I just knew my seat was wet.

"This is Tiff!" Milan announced as he approached with a young white woman. "She's gonna pull your dresses for you."

For the next hour or so, I felt like Cinderella as Tiff dressed me in the prettiest gowns I'd ever seen while my prince sat on the leather couch and gave his input on every outfit. He seemed to enjoy watching me twirl, his eyes fixed on my breasts, my waist, my hips, and of course, my ass. And not to brag, but they're all pretty damn spectacular.

He occasionally gave his opinion, throwing out a "not good enough" or "damn, that looks good on you." One time when they didn't know I was listening, I overheard Milan say "she's beautiful," and Shawn replied, "yeah, she is."

What is happening? It felt like a day out shopping with my boyfriend, only he wasn't my boyfriend, he was a...client? Whatever he was, and whatever I called him, these feelings I was catching were all wrong. Feelings get you dizzy. Feelings make you stupid.

"That's the one," Shawn said of the pale pink sparkly Escada dress that was currently hugging my body. I didn't say anything, but I agreed with him about the dress. It was perfect.

"You really like it?" I asked sweetly.

"I love it."

"That's the one," Milan said, but he didn't count. He was just trying to get his commission. The important thing was that Shawn liked it. And that Shawn was paying for it.

"What about shoes and accessories? And a bag? She needs a clutch," Tiff said, to my delight.

Shawn shrugged. "Y'all are the experts. Give her whatever she needs."

I decided then that he was definitely paying, so I figured why not let him have a tiny taste of things to come. I walked over and stood directly in front of him. "Do you like how it fits?" I asked as I placed his hand on my waist. "Does it seem snug enough right here?"

I could hear his breathing change as he rubbed a finger down toward my hip. "It's perfect," he said, with a hitch in his voice.

That was enough of a taste. I stepped back and turned to walk away so he could get an even better look. As I made my way back into the dressing room, I caught a glimpse of myself in the full length mirror. I looked...dare I say it?

Happy.

10

"I cannot *believe* he bought you red bottoms! Bitch, I'm gagging," Farrah announced as she held the gold Forever Girl to her cheek.

"Excuse you, they're Louboutins," I said cheekily. I was lounging on my bed, basking in the glow of the day before and Farrah was listening to every word with jealousy in her eyes. And who doesn't want to make their friends jealous every now and then? It's delightful.

"What did you do for these? Suck his dick?"

I grabbed my pillow from behind me and threw it at her head. "Nothing. I told you, he knew I needed something to wear for the thing tonight and he took me shopping."

Farrah smelled the shoe and rubbed it on her arm.

"What are you doing?" I asked with a giggle.

"Spreading red bottom dust over myself. I'm claiming mine. I see what the Lord did for you and I want it for myself," she said with her eyes closed.

I shook my head and laughed, but then I started thinking about what she said. I really didn't think the Lord had anything to do with this particular situation. I was raised in the church so I know what the Bible says about these things. Nothing about this was holy.

I put it out of my mind. There was work to be done. It was day 47 of my countdown and I needed to focus. It was gonna take all my energy not to give him some tonight.

"Farrah, I need your advice. Your *serious* advice."

She stopped rubbing herself and frowned. "What's wrong?"

I scrunched up my face in embarrassment. "I'm...attracted to him."

"And that's bad?"

"Yes! Farrah, he is fine. OMG, girl he's so sexy I can't take it. I cannot have sex with this man. I can't. You have to help me!"

She raised her eyebrows. "I love you and everything and you're very pretty but I'm not--"

"No, you nut! Help me, like give me a strategy to keep my legs closed tonight."

"Oh. Girl, that's easy. Don't shave your legs. Or anything else."

"Too late."

"Alright. Umm...wait, why can't you have sex with him?"

"Because, we haven't made an arrangement yet beyond meetings. I'm not having sex until there's an allowance in place. Didn't you read like I told you to?"

She laughed and shook her head. "Can you talk to him about it tonight?"

"No, it's not that kind of environment. It's a benefit, it's this whole thing. It wouldn't feel right."

"I don't know, Mani. If you like him, don't deprive yourself. Be a hoe. Get it how you live."

This was hopeless. She didn't understand because it was a new frontier. I wasn't in a relationship with Shawn. I was in an arrangement, with very real implications and consequences, and I realized at that moment that my mindset, my entire worldview, was shifting. I always thought I knew what normal was, but now? My perception was becoming distorted. And I wasn't sure how I felt about that.

I called to check on Daddy before I started getting ready for the benefit. He seemed to be in good spirits. The surgery was next week, and if things kept going well with my "dates," I would probably be able to take off work and care for him for a couple of days. I owed him that much, and I was looking forward to it.

Right after I hung up with Daddy, Bill texted me. He'd been out of sight, out of mind for me so it was a quick reminder that I needed to do better at my new job.

Hey Beautiful. Just checking in on you.
I hope your day is going well.

Well that was sweet. I replied immediately.
Hi Handsome. I'm doing fine. Thanks for checking
on me. Can't wait until our next meet!

He sent back a smiley face and a wink.

Once we had an arrangement worked out, I was gonna have to keep up with my communication. I didn't foresee it being difficult to juggle both Bill and Shawn, but I needed to stay on top of things so that neither feels neglected. I decided to do a spreadsheet once I had some free time. Getting organized would make things much more efficient.

Now. Let me tell you a little something about Louboutins. Them shits *hurt*.

I'm sure there are some comfortable ones in existence, especially for women who are used to wearing heels. But I wasn't. I thought I was, but these joints are on a whole nother level. And it didn't help that I picked the 100mm. I should have opted for something shorter. Don't get me wrong, they're stunning. Just painful as hell.

I had spent most of the day walking around in them, trying to get acclimated. I did the dishes in them, I took out the trash in them, and I'd even done a few squats in them. Tiff said it takes a while to break in good shoes so maybe they'll actually be comfortable one day. For tonight, though, I was just gonna have to suffer. After all, Grandma Minty always said "beauty is pain."

Farrah did my makeup--gold shadow and highlighter, lashes, blush, and pale pink gloss to match my dress. We debated whether I should wear my hair up or down and in the end, since neither of us are very sophisticated, we did the opposite of what our instincts told us. We did a high bun.

I waited until the very last minute, when the

car was right out front, to put them damn shoes on. The little gold clutch was too small to fit a pair of flip flops so I was doomed to be in pain all night. Hopefully there was seating at the venue.

"You look absolutely gorgeous," Farrah assured me as I buckled the straps. "Take some pics if you can and have fun."

"You didn't tell me not to have sex."

She frowned. "Because I want you to have sex."

"Girl, bye. And thank you for everything," I said as I walked out the door. I walked gingerly toward the black town car and prayed I didn't fall flat on my face.

It wasn't Shawn who met me at the car door, it was an older black gentleman. "Good evening, Miss Imani," he said with a voice as smooth as silk. "I'm Gerald. I'll be your driver for this evening.

"Nice to meet you, Gerald," I said. "Thank you."

He smiled and opened the door for me and I tried to be graceful as I entered but I stumbled a bit. Shawn grabbed my hand as I sat and let out a whistle.

"You look beautiful," he said, and I'm quite sure I actually blushed. He pressed his lips against the back of my hand and smiled. "Thank you for being my date for tonight. I can't promise it will be fun. It's not exactly a night out at the club."

"It's okay. I don't club much anymore," I lied. I was just at Compound a week ago. "So tell me, what can I expect?"

Shawn hesitated. "You want something to drink? Champagne?"

Um, *yeah*. "Yes, please." The girls said to be

polite and demure.

I watched as Shawn poured two glasses of something bubbly. I couldn't see the name on the label and I wanted to ask him what it was but I didn't want to come off like a rube. So I simply sipped, and it was the smoothest, most delicious champagne I've ever tasted. I tried to pace myself but I was done before Shawn even got the bottle back in the cooler.

He took a few sips first, then spoke. "To answer your question, you can expect a lot of bougie people. My parents, my brother, my uncles, basically my whole family minus my sister."

"The bougie people are your family?"

He laughed and took another sip. "I just meant it's a bougie crowd and my family will also be there."

"What are you gonna tell them about me?"

He studied my face. "That I met you at a restaurant and that I enjoy your company."

I was beginning to feel nervous. "Any particular topics I should avoid?"

"It would be nice if you didn't announce your age. Not that you would. Just saying."

"I got you," I said, and he smiled. "Will anyone ask me what I do for a living?"

Shawn thought for a moment. "Probably."

He seemed concerned so I tried to put him at ease. "I'll just tell them I'm working on my MBA."

I could tell he was relieved. "That works."

I smiled and patted his arm. "No worries. It's your night."

He leaned closer. "Did I tell you already that

you look beautiful?"

"You did, but I never get tired of hearing that."

His eyes roamed my body, starting with my lips, down to my neck, my décolletage, my breasts, and then my thighs. He wasn't shy, that's for sure. "Good to know," he said.

The car slowed and finally stopped. "We're here, Mr. Jeter," Gerald called over the seats.

"You ready?" Shawn asked me.

I nodded and prayed I wouldn't make a complete fool of myself in my brand new red bottoms. My feet hurt already and I had only taken a car ride.

Gerald opened Shawn's door first, and Shawn walked around and waited while Gerald opened my door. Shawn held out his hand and I grabbed it. Getting out of the car proved even harder than getting in, and I almost took a header right onto the pavement. Shawn held me up with his strong arms and saved me from embarrassment.

"I got you," he said. "Just follow my lead."

We made our way into the venue and I realized I was in the ballroom of the Wellington Hotel. That part wasn't new to me; I've been to weddings and the occasional banquet in hotel. It was the crowd that was different.

The best way I can describe it is that everyone looked like money. While I was teetering around on my brand new Louboutins, these women glided atop their own as if they had been born in them. My soles were still shiny, still uniformly red, but their soles bore the scars of wear and tear from years of charity galas and expensive dinners and trips around the world. Sure, my brand new Escada dress sparkled perfectly and my little Loeffler Randall clutch was dainty and stylish, but it was just a costume to me. For these ladies, it was a wardrobe. A lifestlye.

I'd gone home last night after our field trip to Saks and googled the names of the labels on my new items. Just out of curiosity. I was flattered that Shawn spent that much money on me, but also a bit embarrassed by how little I really knew about nice clothes. I always thought anything that had some cotton in it was good quality. And not that expensive equals quality necessarily but it was certainly much better made than anything in my meager closet.

At any rate, we entered the ballroom and were greeted by everyone we passed. Shawn was, anyway. I smiled and tried not to stand out.

An older couple approached us. The woman had a smile on her face but the man just stared blankly. He looked a lot like Shawn, who leaned over and whispered in my ear. "Here come my parents."

11

Mrs. Jeter was a tiny woman but there was strength behind her eyes. We all know the type. She greeted me warmly but with some distance, not offering me a hug as is custom among most southern women. "Nice to meet you, Imani," she said with a squeeze of her hand around mine. I returned the sentiment and she looked at her son. "Shawn, she's gorgeous. Where have you been hiding her?"

Shawn chuckled. "And this is my pops. Mr. Dennis Jeter."

"Nice to meet you, Mr. Jeter," I said. He nodded but didn't address me at all. He seemed stern and rigid, like he'd be absolutely no fun at all to be around.

"Young lady, do you mind if I steal your date for a moment?" he finally said to me.

"Of course not," I said with a smile. The two men walked away and I stood there with his mother, feeling awkward and uncomfortable.

"Are you enjoying yourself so far?" she asked. Her face was slightly wrinkled but still very pretty. She'd let her grey come in fully and it made her look regal.

"Oh, we just got here. But the venue is beautiful."

She eyed me carefully and thoroughly. "Have you eaten yet, dear?"

"I haven't, actually."

"Come with me. We have a beautiful spread in here," she said as she hooked her arm in mine. We walked across the ballroom together and I worried that Shawn wouldn't be able to find me. But I forgot all about him when I saw the tables of food.

Mrs. Jeter wasn't lying. It was beautiful. Rack of lamb, roast beef, roast chicken, and meatballs swimming in a dark sauce. There was also a table full of side dishes and breads, a sushi station, a pasta station, troughs full of pink shrimp on sparkling white ice, a long tray of grilled salmon topped with onions and glaze, and an entire table just for several different types of caviar.

Just for a second, I wondered if these people actually ate but one glance around the room answered my question. As beautiful and elegant as this crowd was, they still had one thing in common with me. They eat when hungry. Calories be damned.

I procured a modest helping of salmon and steamed vegetables to start with. That seemed like a classy choice for a first trip. Mrs. Jeter got down and dirty with her plate, telling the chefs to pile her plate up with chicken, lamb, mac and cheese, greens, and buttered rolls. I followed her back to her--I mean *our*-- table and set my plate down. We passed a bar on our way there so I planned to circle back and get myself a drink. But before I could, Shawn tapped me on the shoulder.

"What do you want from the bar?"

"You read my mind," I said. "White Zinfandel."

He nodded and walked away leaving me alone with his mother again. I couldn't think of anything to say to her so I simply commenced to stuffing my face.

I was halfway through my salmon course when Mr. Jeter took his seat next to his wife. He was empty-handed and seemed irritated. She was too busy eating to notice so he simply sat there sulking.

Shawn brought my drink and when he sat down, it was like a switch had flipped in Mr. Jeter. He set his sights on me. "So, Imani. What do you do?" he asked.

"I'm a student, actually. Working on my MBA."

"Ohhhhh," the Jeter parents said in unison. The tone was one of sheer delight. "Which school?" Mrs. Jeter asked.

"Georgia State."

"Ohhhh," they said again, but this time, the tone was unmistakable: disappointment. You would have thought I told them I killed their damn dog or something.

It bugged me. For some strange reason, I wanted to make a good impression. I wanted them to like me. "I'm planning to go into real estate," I said proudly. But only Mrs. Jeter perked up at that.

"Good for you!" she said. "Did Shawn tell you he went to Howard? And Carnegie Mellon?"

"She knows, Ma," Shawn said.

"I'm so proud of him. I'm proud of all my kids,"

she said, and the bit at the end made me smile. She wasn't in any danger of being accused of favoritism, at least not by me, but it's one of those things mothers have to say just to make sure you know.

"I can see why," I said, and Mrs. Jeter beamed.

Mr. Jeter continued to study me. "What made you decide on Georgia State?"

"Pop," Shawn said, his tone sounding like a warning.

"I'm making conversation," Mr. Jeter said.

"It's okay. Um, I wanted to be close to my parents. My father is on disability and I have two younger brothers. I like being able to help out when they need me."

Mrs. Jeter looked at her husband in triumph and I knew I was missing something. "Good for you," she said to me. "Children *should* take care of their elders. That's how our people do, anyway. We don't believe in nursing homes and such."

I nodded at her and continued eating, and that was how the rest of the meal went. People came by the table in a constant stream to speak to and flatter the Jeters. If I didn't know anything about them, the attention they received would make it clear that they were important.

Shawn was quiet beside me and I wondered if something was wrong. Then I figured it was time to earn my keep. "Hey," I said to him. "You okay?"

"I'm good," he said as he stabbed his fork into a slice of roast beef.

"Did I tell you how handsome you look tonight?" I teased, and that got a smile out of him. He really did look insanely good in his black tuxedo. "We could be the prom king and queen."

He laughed at my corny joke and raised his eyebrows as he leaned closer to my ear. "You know what happens after prom, right?"

I didn't say anything and his face fell. "I'm sorry. That was too much."

"No, it's not that," I said. I wasn't offended at all. Just surprised by how turned on that made me. "You just caught me off guard."

He glanced down at my plate. "Did you get enough to eat?"

"I think so."

"Did you see the dessert station?"

"Shawn, I'm good. I promise. But you're sweet."

He smiled. "Just making sure you're straight."

I smiled back but our eye-flirting was interrupted by this...this...okay, the best way to describe her would be to call her The Blasian Amazon. Seriously, she had to be close to six feet tall with a gorgeous face and a perfect body. I'm no slouch but DAMN.

Mr. Jeter perked up. "Joya!" he exclaimed, before jumping up to hug her. "How long has it been, young lady?"

Joya the Blasian Amazon smiled and revealed two rows of perfect white teeth. "At least two years."

Mr. Jeter nudged Shawn. "You see this, Shawn? Look who turned up!"

Shawn rolled his eyes at me before standing to

his feet. He hugged Joya and kissed her cheek and I felt...some kind of way.

"Good to see you," he said politely. She smiled in such a way that I knew they were familiar with each other. *Very* familiar.

Why does it matter? You're at work, I reminded myself.

"Tell Shawn what you've been up to," Mr. Jeter instructed without a hint of subtlety.

Joya smiled again. "I got hired on at Johnson and McDonald."

Shawn raised his perfect eyebrows. "Nice! Good for you, I remember you saying they were your top choice."

She beamed at that. "I can't believe you remembered that."

"Oh, Joya Owens, this is my date, Imani Emerson."

I smiled up at her from the comfort of my seat. "Nice to meet you."

"You too," she said with a smile that belonged in a Colgate commercial. I didn't detect an edge in her voice. She seemed genuinely nice, and that pissed me off. Now I couldn't think mean things about her.

I assumed she was Mr. Jeter's pick, and I have to admit, no matter how many times I told myself this was work, it felt good that I was Shawn's.

12

Joya eventually made her way back to wher-
ever she came from--to Mr. Jeter's disappointment--
and Shawn was called to the stage to speak.

"Good evening everyone. It's amazing to look
out here and see so many beautiful faces. Some of you
I know very well, and others of you I hope to know
better. But I thank you for showing up tonight for a
cause that is near and dear to my heart."

He paused and waited for the projection to hit
the screen. The first picture was of a young woman
lying in a hospital bed. "This is my beloved sister
Erica Jeter-Harris."

There were some awws from the crowd. The
slideshow continued, showing Erica as a young cheer-
leader, then a majorette, then a couple of print ads for
Sears, which got a lot of laughs. Good-natured laughs
at her 80s hairstyle and the terrible clothes. Shawn
watched with love in his eyes, laughing at some of the
pics and looking melancholy at others. Interspersed
throughout were pictures of her lying in bed or on the
couch, all a stark contrast from the pics of her when
she was healthy.

Shawn continued. "Erica wanted to be here tonight but she wasn't up to it. She was my inspiration for Safe Cell for obvious reasons. Those pictures tell quite a story, right? My sister has always been a vibrant, outgoing young woman with big dreams, but it seemed to me like her illness was always waiting, lurking in the shadows, ready to take her down any moment. And that's what sickle cell anemia does. It robs otherwise healthy people of time. Time to run, time to play, time to sing and dance. Time to learn."

He paused as the final picture appeared on the screen. It was Erica holding twin babies with her husband by her side. "And time to be a mother or a father. My sister's biggest fear is that she won't get the chance to see her daughters graduate from college and get married and have babies of their own, and--" he trailed off and looked down. I heard sniffles in the crowd and when Shawn wiped his eyes, tears welled up in my eyes, as well.

I felt like an intruder. This was obviously very personal to the Jeter family and here I was, their son's *literal* escort who otherwise wouldn't have been within twenty miles of an event like this.

Shawn cleared his throat. "Here's what we know about sickle cell: 1 in 500 in five African Americans is born with the disease. That's a very high rate relative to other groups. We also know that there is no cure, so children with the disease learn how to manage the symptoms which are often debilitating. Now, I'm no scientist. I don't know how to conduct the research necessary to cure this. But I do know how to fund it. And that's why we're here. Many of you have been touched by this disease in some way. Others of you feel strongly about finding a cure. Whatever the reason you're here, you're *here*. And I, along with the rest of the board of directors, would like to give our most heartfelt thank you to you for your presence and your contribution. Now, the bar is open, the music will play, and we've still got several items up for auction. Let's do this, y'all."

Everyone applauded enthusiastically. Most of all me. I was proud of him. Which is weird because I barely knew this man. But I was proud. And impressed.

He made his way back to the table and extended his hand. "Let's go spend my money," he said, and I was delighted to do so.

"Your speech was amazing," I said as we walked. Well, he walked. I teetered. "I can tell you're passionate about this. That's so commendable."

"Thank you," he said without looking at me.

"Your sister is lucky to have a brother like you."

He didn't respond but he did squeeze my hand.

We made our way through the crowd, although we got stopped several times so that people could hug him or congratulate him or send well wishes to Erica. By the time we got to the auction tables, I felt like I was walking on knives. Damn Louboutins. I was starting to think the bottoms are red to hide the blood.

"Alright, Miss Imani. What should I bid on?"

I'd never been to a silent auction but I have spent plenty of money on shit I didn't need so this was right up my alley. I perused the items and read each placard carefully. The luxury spa weekend at Chateau Elan started at $1,500. An autographed Atlanta Falcons football opened at $500. A catered dinner party for six with a private chef started at $4,500. The highest bid on a pair of diamond stud earrings was $3,200. A boat called Bayliner was--I couldn't believe my eyes--$430,000. And there were actual bids on it!

"I found it," I teased. "You should get this boat. The price seems reasonable."

Shawn looked over my shoulder. "That's because it's an older model."

"Oh. Right," I said, like I would know. "I'm sure you already have one anyway, right?"

He smiled and raised his eyebrows and I laughed. He definitely wasn't a braggart, I had to give him that much. "You like to fish?" he asked me.

My daddy used to beg me to go with him and my brothers and I always refused. Now he didn't ask anymore. "I love to fish," I said.

"I'll take you out some time," he said as he eyed a golf package. "See anything you like? Don't be shy."

"I thought that spa weekend looked pretty nice."

He reached into his suit pocket and produced a gorgeous woodgrain pen. "Put in a bid. And don't be timid. You gotta be aggressive to get what you want," he said.

"Do you usually get what you want?"

He eyed me suggestively. "I *always* get what I want."

A tingle crawled up my spine and I turned and walked away before I got into trouble. I thought about what I should bid on the spa package--up to $2,100 now--and finally settled on an even $3,000. I had no idea what I was doing but Shawn said to be aggressive.

At the end of the evening, I was happy to learn I won the spa weekend. Or *we* won, depending on if he wanted to go. If not, I was taking Farrah. Shawn congratulated me and Mrs. Jeter smiled at me and told me she hopes I enjoy it. Even Mr. Jeter managed a smile, although he didn't say anything.

Later, in the car, Shawn seemed distracted.

"Hey," I said, "are you okay?"

He sighed and stared out the window at the passing cars. "I wish my sister could have made it tonight."

It was a delicate subject but I was actually starting to feel invested. "How is she doing right now?"

He shook his head. "She's suffering. It's very painful, when the episodes start. And she doesn't like taking meds so..." he trailed off.

I grabbed his hand and squeezed it. "I'm sorry," was all I could think to say. He squeezed my hand in return and we rode in silence for a while.

"So I've seen where you live. Do you wanna see where I live?" he asked.

I answered without even thinking, "Yes!"

We continued holding hands and I thought about my next move. I decided that the spa package was more than I would have made tonight anyway, even if I had sex with him, which I really wanted to do. That said, it wasn't cash, and I couldn't lose sight of the fact that my goal is money for school, not luxury experiences.

"We're here," Shawn said as the car slowed. I looked up and saw a gate opening slowly to allow us in. The driveway was long and winding and surrounded by trees and shrubbery.

When we finally pulled up to the house, I was a little disappointed. It wasn't the grand estate I had been expecting. Don't get me wrong, it was nice. It was a bright white Colonial with navy blue shutters. The main building was flanked by two smaller buildings, one of which housed a two-car garage. Only two cars. My spidey senses started tingling.

But then we walked in the front door.

My eyes took in the sights, and there was so much to see. The coffered ceilings, the picture window in the living room, the two story marble fireplace, the beautiful deep brown textured wood floors, the artwork. It was a feast for the eyes. Absolutely gorgeous.

While I was staring at the house, he was staring at me. "You want some wine? Or I could have a drink mixed for you."

"Oh no, I'm fine."

"Yes, you are."

I giggled and looked around. "Wait, did you say have a drink mixed for me? Is someone else here?"

"Yeah. I have a few staff members who are always around."

I really wanted to ask him how rich he was but I'm sure that was poor form. Instead, I asked a less personal question. "How many acres are you sitting on?"

"Seven and some change."

"Nice," I said. "Are you gonna give me the grand tour or are we just gonna stand here in the foyer?"

He smiled and looked down at my feet. "You wanna take your shoes off, don't you?"

"What gave me away?"

"Them wobbly ass ankles."

I smacked his arm and he laughed, the sound echoing throughout the large foyer. He led me to a bench and sat me down. He knelt in front of me and removed my painful shoes, his fingers lightly grazing my feet and ankles and sending little shocks through my body. Once my shoes were removed, I tried my hardest not to sigh in relief. He stood and held out his hand and I grabbed it and stood in front of him. At that moment, I decided I was ready to kiss him. The sexual tension was driving me insane.

I stared in his eyes, daring him to make a move. He placed his hand on my lower back, right at the top of my ass, teasing, making me want him even more. I leaned in and just before our lips met, he pulled back.

Ouch.

"Shit. Imani, I need to tell you something before this goes any further."

So he was a Splenda Daddy after all. FML. Whose house was this? Whose money had he spent yesterday? It was day 47. I did not have time for this bullshit.

"What is it?" I asked, taking a few steps backward.

"I wanted to tell you this yesterday but we just...clicked. And the vibe was so good. It was natural, and I didn't wanna fuck that up. But now..."

I knew it was too good to be true. I was angry at myself for letting my feelings override my common sense. Lesson learned.

"Okay, here's the thing. We've met before."

"That's it?" I asked, somewhat relieved.

"Yeah. At Port. The day that guy was messing with you. I was the guy in the hat."

My mouth dropped open. My knight. How? "I don't understand. How did you find me?"

He looked at the floor in embarrassment. "I overhead you talking to your boss and I don't know what made me do it but on a whim, I signed up to a couple of sites hoping I would see you on there."

"Why the hell didn't you just ask me out at Port? That's fucking weird!"

"I know. I can see how that must look to you. I don't know why I didn't ask you out that day. Actually, I'm lying. I do know. I thought it was bad timing. And that maybe I was too old for you."

"Did you suddenly get younger, or was this the perfect way to trick me into going out with you?"

"No, I--you're right. It was wrong. I wasn't thinking. I just...I met you and you were so...there's really no excuse. I see that. Just tell me how to make it up to you and I will. Anything."

"Take me home. Now."

"Imani--"

"No. Take me home."

He was speechless and I was ready to fight if need be. But in the end, he did as I asked. We didn't speak on the way to my place and I silently cursed myself for letting him know where I lived on the second day. I got caught up. It would never happen again. Lesson learned.

We pulled up and I put my hand on the door, not even caring to wait for him to open it. He put a hand on my arm to stop me.

"At least let me pay you for your time. I owe you that much."

True.

He pulled three hundreds from his wallet and placed them in my outstretched palm. I stuffed it in my bra and opened the door. I got out and just before I closed the door behind me, I told him.

"This is over. Don't contact me ever again."

13

Shawn

I know how this looks but chill for a second and let me explain, alright?

I saw her at Port, this lovely, brown, thick, shapely human specimen, and I was immediately drawn to her. I watched her serve drinks and deliver plates. Actually, I was watching her ass most of the time, and the sway of her hips as she glided past my table.

I see beautiful women all the time, and I can't even say there was something special about this one at first glance. But then I heard her laughing and joking with the customers and I was taken by her wit. She was sharp, and her confidence level was on a thousand. Sexy as hell.

I'm used to getting what I want so I formulated a plan to get her phone number before I left. But then that Bubba in a business suit started bothering her, and of course I stepped in, because that's what a man is supposed to do. But afterward, I knew my plan was foiled. It would have been in extremely poor taste to try to push up on her right after she was basically assaulted.

So what did I do? Probably the next worse thing. I listened in on her conversation and got another bright idea. Mind you, I already had an account at Top Shelf. I didn't know for sure she'd use that one but it's the biggest and the best so I may have logged on every day until her profile popped up. Okay, I definitely did that. What can I say? I'm used to getting what I want.

By the way, I'm Shawn Jeter. My government is Rayshawn but Shawn goes over better in the business world. Yeah, I'm an executive and all but I still have to deal with other types of people and I know exactly how they think.

I kinda half-ass fell into this job if I'm being honest. My father and uncle founded Northstar Capital, one of the largest black owned real estate investment groups in the country, and I was groomed from an early age to become a full participant in the family business. I went to B school, got an internship, the whole nine, and when my father retires, he plans to put me in charge. As a managing partner, I have a lot to do but it doesn't fund my life. I have a healthy trust fund I haven't had to touch yet because much of personal income comes from investments. I got into crypto early and let's just say Bitcoin has been *very* good to me.

Anyway, I only stopped by Port that day because I had a meeting with a contractor at a property nearby and the receptionist suggested it. I'm not gonna say it was fate but I'm glad she led me to that spot at that time. Too bad it was all for nothing.

"Leaving early today, Boss?" Dita asked as I passed her desk. She stays in my business.

I checked my watch and frowned. "It's after 3. I can't be sitting in Atlanta traffic every day. You know I hate that."

She sighed and cut her eyes at me. "Do I need to cancel anything or did you at least take care of your obligations first?"

At least. She was the only person in this whole damn place I let talk to me like that. I inherited her from my father when he hired a new admin and she treats me like a son who gets on her nerves. But sometimes she brings me home cooked meals and that makes up for it.

I sat on the edge of her desk. "You don't have to cancel anything but I do need you to put in an order for me. For flowers."

Dita snickered. "What's this one's name?"

"Why you being so mean today? Did Horace stay out all night again?"

She slapped my arm and pointed her finger right in my face. "Don't be talking about my husband, hear?"

"I told you if you get in my business I'mma get in yours."

She held out a post-it pad and a pen. "Write down the information for me and then get out of here and leave me alone." She punctuated her statement wink and I flashed a smile back.

Dita's an old-school southern black woman and you know what that means. She wants me to get married and have some babies because apparently it's unnatural for a grown man of means not to have a family. And I admit, being a single and childless man in the corporate world is not seen as an asset. It's like people don't trust you. And that's the hill my father has chosen to die on. I won't get the big job without a wife.

I know it kills my big brother that they chose me. He's 41 years old with a wife, three kids, and a dog. He is the literal personification of the American Dream, the firstborn son, and Pop's namesake, and yet my father and my uncle prefer me. It's a long story I've never heard but I still know it won't have a happy ending.

As far as marriage and kids, I think it's too late for me. What I look like dealing with teenagers when I'm in my 50? Nah, I'm good on that.

I will say this though: It's a strange feeling to have everything you could ever want and not have anyone to share it with or pass it on to. My little sister has twin girls and my brother has a daughter and two sons. I suppose I can leave my earthly treasures to them when I go, but it feels like a waste not to create another me. I'm pretty damn cool.

I look good, too. No sense denying it. And it's gotten me a whole lotta ass over the years. But that gets tiresome sometimes. I've dated women my own age, slightly older, and various ranges of younger, and I can never seem to find everything I want in the same package. When I registered at Top Shelf, that was me looking for a one-stop-shop. They got some baddies on that site, no question, but I wasn't interested.

The whole sugar baby aspect of it didn't really register until Imani brought it up. I'm not even gonna front. I've gone to Brazil and the Dominican Republic with my homeboys, so I'm not above coming out of my pocket. But for some odd reason the whole website aspect felt grimy to me, allowances and paid meetings on an ongoing basis.

Until Imani.

She had it all. Looks, brains, ambition, and a little bit of an edge. She struck me as someone like myself, a person who will bend the rules when necessary to get what she wants. That's why I thought she'd understand why I did what I did.

In hindsight, I can see how I came off. Not good.

I drove down Peachtree with the windows down blasting Kendrick Lamar. It was that kinda day. I had a meeting with my pops at my parents' house and I was psyching myself up for what was coming.

Joya.

My old man's been beating that drum for years. I met her in undergrad and we spent a little time together here and there. Okay, we hooked up. But she had set her sights higher than little old me and I moved on. We're friends on social media so I've been aware of her comings and goings since graduation but I'm not sure when she crossed paths with my father. All I know is that last night was all his doing.

I pulled in through the gate and sped up the

windy road to the house. I parked next to his silver Mercedes and took a deep breath.

Adelle, our longtime cleaning lady, greeted me with a hug when I let myself in. "Good to see your handsome face around here," she said with a grin, showing off that open-face gold tooth I used to obsess over when I was little.

"You just saw me on the fourth, Della."

"I did? Oh, that's right. Della's getting old, baby." That was her running joke, only it wasn't funny anymore. It was true.

"Pop!" I called.

"In here!" he answered from the kitchen.

He was seated at the island eating a bologna sandwich. No matter how wealthy he got, he still ate the same lunch every day.

We hugged and I grabbed a beer from the fridge. "Last night went well," I announced.

"Oh yeah? What's the final tally?"

I shrugged. "I don't have a number but we got expenses down to a little over 50 percent. Last year we were at 64 percent," I added quickly, hoping to head off any negativity. "I should have a number before the end of the week."

Pop nodded and bit into his sandwich. I watched him chew slowly and for several seconds longer than seemed normal to me. It was a reminder that he was getting older, just like Della, and my mother. You forget that your beloved elders will leave you until you watch them in action. It's enough to make you weep if you let yourself really think about it. So I don't think about it.

"What did you wanna talk to me about," I asked.

Pop set his sandwich on his plate and pointed at the water cooler. I grabbed a glass and filled it for him and he took several gulps before finally speaking.

"That young lady you brought with you last night. Is that serious?"

"She was just a date, Pop."

"How did you meet her?"

"At a restaurant downtown."

"Which restaurant?"

I stared at him and frowned. "Why are you asking me all these questions?"

"Are you new?" he asked, and despite the sharpness in his tone, I laughed. Because I was not, in fact, new to this shit at all.

"We're friends. That's all."

He nodded. "That's good. Friendship is important."

I stared at him, my patience wearing thin. "What's on your mind, Pop?"

"Same thing that's been on my mind for ten years. You need a family."

"I have a family."

"A family of your *own*, boy. How do you expect to carry on my legacy without one?"

"DJ has a family. Erica has a family."

"Stop deflecting."

"I'm not deflecting. I just--"

"Randall is in agreement with me on this. The company goes to you. I'd think you would be grateful but maybe I'm missing something. I don't know."

"I'm grateful, Pop. I just--"

"You're loyal to your brother. I get that. But this is business, not personal."

I nodded and pretended I was placated and Pop went back to his sandwich as if it was settled. DJ wasn't perfect but he was as qualified as I was. More, even. His MBA came from Tuck and he has almost three years of experience on me. My father's preference for me wasn't based on business at all. It was hella personal, and we both knew it. But he has never told me why.

"It was nice seeing Joya last night, wasn't it?" he said, finally dropping the hammer.

"I guess."

Pop sighed and shook his head. "Let's cut the bullshit. Give me one good reason why you aren't interested."

"I knew that was coming."

He raised his left eyebrow, a move I knew all too well. "And yet you didn't have an answer prepared? That was poor planning on your part."

"What do you want me to say, Pop? She's smart and beautiful and all that but I don't know if I can see myself married to her."

"That's not a reason."

I crossed my arms and frowned like a little boy in trouble. Nothing I said would make a lick of difference so why bother arguing?

Pop was undeterred. "If you're waiting until you fall in love you might as well just marry the first pretty young thing with a cute face and a tiny waist."

I rolled my eyes.

"I know your taste," he said.

"Pop, I understand where you're coming from. I'm not ready."

"You're almost a 40-year-old man, boy! What the hell are you waiting for?"

I uncrossed my arms and wiped a hand across my eyes. "What's wrong with Joya that she's not married. Huh? She's the same age as me. You ever think about that?"

Pop narrowed his eyes. "Don't think I don't know what you're doing."

I smiled involuntarily. "What am I doing, Pop?"

"You know, and you know *I* know. That's why you're smiling."

"I'm not smiling," I said, and then I laughed.

He leaned closer to me, and with a lowered voice, he said, "you feel guilty that I picked you over DJ so you're trying to sabotage your own life to make yourself a less attractive candidate."

The smile fell from my face and he nodded in triumph. "If anybody should feel guilty, it's me. And I don't. So why are you carrying that? DJ made poor choices and he has to live with the consequences."

"What choices?"

Pop stared at me and there was sadness behind those eyes. "Don't concern yourself."

He said that every time I asked and it never satisfied me. I was very concerned.

14

I've had my heart broken before. My first love, Quincy Williams, cheated on me with Tyshanna Hart. Cheating is hurtful enough, but he made it even worse by cheating with a girl I hated, the girl who had beaten me for homecoming queen. I lost almost ten pounds mourning that relationship. Lovesick. That's how I know something happens to us physically when our emotions are out of whack.

You can imagine my surprise when I woke up on day 45 feeling off. Not broken-hearted like I was with Quincy because that would be ridiculous. But I was emotionally out of sorts. It confused me because I barely knew Shawn. It made no sense at all.

I blocked him as soon as I got home the night of the gala. I'm not gonna pretend to be shocked that someone on the internet turned out to be a creep but for some reason, I thought he was--well, something other than what he showed me that night. It was a shame, too. I hadn't had sex since Cal and the spark between us was undeniable. That smile. Those lips...

Oh well. I still had Bill on the hook and tuition wasn't going to pay itself. I texted him last night to let him know I was looking forward to our date. He responded immediately.

I can't wait to see you. Don't forget to pick a spot. Anywhere you want.

I texted back a smiley face but that little emoji couldn't have been further from the truth of my actual mood. Farrah listened to my complaints about Shawn and she was supportive, as always. But I still couldn't stop thinking about it. Shawn was the Knight. My knight. But he had done the most unknightly thing ever and practically stalked me and then lied by omission because he knew he was wrong. I don't care how fine he was. There was no coming back from that.

He even had the nerve to send me apology flowers. They were beautiful, but still. That was done.

But I couldn't think about any of that now. They were prepping my daddy for surgery and I was in the hospital waiting room, cold and exhausted from my double shift the day before. Fran was still in the dark about my new venture but she told me I seemed less weighed down than I was before. I guess that was a good thing.

"Mama, relax," Omari said. "You're bout to jump out your skin."

My mother stopped tapping her foot like a jackhammer and smiled. A sad smile. "I'm sorry. I'm on edge. I shouldn't have had three cups of coffee."

We all knew she was worrying herself sick about my daddy. She never let herself be true to her emotions. If she let herself get upset, it could never be about what we thought it was about. It always had to be something else, something trivial, a minor annoyance. She wears the mask and it exhausts *me*. I don't know how she does it.

"Did you eat anything before you came?" I asked her.

"Who can eat?" she answered. "I'll have something once I know he's okay."

I nodded and tried not to think about what would happen if he ended up not being okay. I stood and unwrapped the purple chenille blanket from around me and laid it over my mother. She nodded her gratitude.

I was walking over to the vending machine when my phone vibrated in my pocket. I checked and it was Bill asking how my day was going. I don't know what made me do it given how new our situation was, but I confessed that I was at the hospital for my daddy's surgery. He asked me if I was okay and I responded the best way I knew how:

I'm trying to be.

Daddy went under around 1 o'clock in the afternoon. We began to get antsy around 4 o'clock, and at 4:10, the doctor finally came out to speak to us.

"Mrs. Emerson. Your husband is awake and things went well."

My mother exhaled in relief. "Thank God."

"You can go in and see him. Don't be alarmed if he starts vomiting. It's a perfectly normal reaction to anesthesia for some patients."

She nodded. "Is he awake?"

"He's in and out. Come on, I'll show you the way."

We walked down the hallways, past scared family members and busy nurses. A custodian mopped up something or other and a toddler climbed on a chair without a care in the world.

I hate hospitals.

Dr. Johnson stopped in front of room 238 and we followed him inside.

I was used to seeing a big teddy bear of a man when I looked at my daddy, but in that hospital bed, in his pale blue gown, a plastic yellow bowl beside him to catch his vomit, Daddy looked helpless and frail. It was a jarring visual, and it made the tears pour out of me like a rainstorm. My daddy didn't look like my daddy anymore.

My mother approached him slowly. "William?"

Daddy looked but didn't seem to see us at first. Then it was like he woke up from a dream. "Sarita," he said.

She leaned over and kissed his forehead. "How are you feeling?"

"Sick."

"See?" said Dr. Johnson. "Perfectly normal. I'm gonna get out of your hair but buzz the nurse if you need anything."

I let Omari and Giovanni hug Daddy first, and

then I pounced on him. Carefully, of course. He stroked my hair. "Y'all act like I'm dying. I'm fine," he said into my shoulder.

Just then, a nurse entered the room with a large bouquet of flowers and a gift basket.

"What's all this?" my mother asked. "You got a secret admirer out there, William?"

Omari took the gift basket from the nurse and examined it. "This has all kinda meat and cheese in it. And chocolate too!"

"It's beautiful," my mother said. "Is there a card?"

Omari turned the basket around in his arms and searched. "Not on this. Mani, check the flowers."

I stood and walked over to the table. The flowers were exquisite. I couldn't contain my shock when I flipped the card over:

GET WELL SOON. BILL

15

Shawn

I've dated a lot of women. A LOT. I don't say that to brag; I'm just making the important point that I'm not hurting for female attention.

I know I owe some of my success with women to my success in business, but I'm not hurting in the looks department either. The combination of the two is an aphrodisiac because let's face it: women crave security. It's primal.

I always laugh at those tv shows and movies that have a billionaire or a prince who pretends to be poor to make sure the woman he likes really wants him for who he is. Because real talk, no man with money actually plays them prince and pauper games in real life. We want topnotch women, the type who have enough sense and pride to care about how a relationship benefits them. All these chicks out here running from relationship to relationship without giving it any thought past charm and dick size are bottom-of-the-barrel and stupid, I don't care how fine they are.

I did that once with this slim goody from Birmingham named Anika. She kept making a point to tell me she didn't care about my money. She even tried to split the check with me every time we went out. I was young--mid 20s--and hadn't figured it all out yet, and from my inexperienced point of view, she was either a feminist or a control freak. In hindsight, I see her for what she actually was--stupid.

I've been in love before, I think. Who knows what that really means, anyway? What I can tell you is that her name was Taylor Meeks and we dated for two years. My mother set that whole thing up. She had everything a good boy like me would want in a woman. She went to Spelman, pledged AKA, got her MBA from Columbia, and had already started her career as a healthcare administrator when we started dating. She was attractive, although not as much ass as I usually like. But that's just window dressing, and the rest of her was fine.

I don't know what happened there. Okay, I'm lying. I cheated on her, and she was right to leave. I was past old enough to know better, but I still pouted and sulked like I was the victim. I actually shed a few thug tears over her and sat around listening to "Kiss and Say Goodbye" and shit. Last I heard, she was married to a surgeon and living in Chicago. I bear her no ill will. I'm happy she's happy. She was a good woman and she deserved it.

Then there was Tashka Brown, a brickhouse with a PhD in public health, daughter of Vernon Brown, owner and CEO of one of the oldest insurance companies in the South. We actually went ring shopping and Pop couldn't have been happier, for once. Mr. Brown agreed when I asked for his blessing and I had a proposal date all set. It all went to hell when she abruptly broke up with me to move across the country for a consulting job. I can admit it: I was heartbroken. And she never really gave me a reason. She just said she needed to focus on her career. As if I was a distraction and not the love of her life. I spent almost a month mourning her. Drinking, smoking weed, and listening to "Kiss and Say Goodbye."

After Tashka, I commenced to womanizing and Pop commenced to judging me. It was a cliché and I'm not proud of it, but it was how I chose to deal with my pain. Once I hit 34, I came to my senses and slowed my roll. I didn't think I'd fall in love again but I assumed I'd eventually meet someone I liked enough to actually settle down with.

There was a knock at my office door. I quickly paused the music coming from my computer and said, "come in."

Nita walked in a dropped a stack of papers on my desk. "I need you to sign off on these before I file them."

I frowned as I flipped through the thick packet. "This is ridiculous."

"Agreed."

"Give me another day. I'm in the middle of something."

Nita rolled her eyes. "I thought we were going paperless."

"We are. Eventually. Pop is old-school, you know that."

"Just put 'em on my desk when you're done," she called as she walked out.

I already had a consultant in mind and I'd priced the equipment, training, and hours it would take to make the switch. The hardest part was convincing Pop that it will save the company money in the long run. And I low-key believe it's more about sentiment for him than anything else. He hates change, especially technological change. He'd once remarked to me with a sad look on his face, "the world is leaving me behind."

When I get the big job, it will be the first thing I do. *If* I get the big job, that is.

Nita had left the door cracked. I walked over and closed it before returning to my desk. I hit play and went back to work as "Kiss and Say Goodbye" played on loop.

I met Mama for lunch at Hybrid, this cool little Soul Food/Latin fusion spot. Mrs. Julia Jeter is a lady who lunches and she's never without her pearls and red lipstick but in her heart of hearts, she's just a southern girl who loves to eat.

I showed up at 1 on the dot and she showed up five minutes late, as always, so she could make an entrance. I kissed her cheek and she air kissed mine (can't mess up the lipstick).

"So what's this all about?" she asked once we were seated. She hadn't even picked up her menu yet.

She'd seen me coming.

"I need some advice."

"Well, obviously. What about?"

I chuckled. "Let's wait until you have your wine."

"Boy," she said with a laugh. But she didn't disagree. And ten minutes later, a glass of Rose safely in hand, she blinked those long lashes at me and implored me to speak my mind.

I took a deep breath. "Okay, here's my question. What do you do if you mess up with somebody you care about?"

She sat there quietly. My mother thinks like most people watch tv. It's like she can see every angle clearly in her mind and has to choose the right dialogue for her role in the scene. "Is this about that young lady you brought with you the other day?"

"I plead the fifth on that one. This is strictly rhetorical."

"Well, it's been my experience that when your daddy gets on my bad side, he always makes it up to me with a gift."

I sliced the cornbread and slathered it in honey butter. "So throw money at it?"

"That's what your daddy does." She lowered her voice. "But it doesn't necessarily take all that."

"What does it take?"

She was thinking again. "Genuine acknowledgment of your mistake and the fact that you feel bad about it." She sipped her wine. "Do you?"

I didn't even have to think about it. "I do."

"Then make that clear to her." She fingered her wedding band. "All the gifts in the world don't mean a damn thing if you're not really sorry. And we always know it."

There was a bit of an edge in her voice when she spoke that last sentence. "You okay?" I asked.

She blinked rapidly. "Why wouldn't I be?"

I decided to leave it alone. "No reason."

"You talk to your sister today?"

"Not yet. I'm headed over there after work. Why? She okay?"

"Oh yes, she's feeling better. Todd and the girls are taking good care of her."

I nodded. My mother stared at me again with those eyes, the ones that were always able to read my every thought somehow. No sense in pretending. "What did you think of Imani?"

Mama smiled. "She seemed a little young. How old is she?"

Shit. "Twenty-five."

"I trust that you know your father will not be pleased."

I nodded again.

"But I'm not him. All I've ever wanted was for my children to be happy. If she makes you happy, then I'm content."

The waitress brought our food. Mama had the fried chicken quesadillas and I settled on the Cajun shrimp empanadas. Just before she took a bite, Mama reached over a touched my hand. "Just do me one favor. Don't mess this one up."

16

Imani

Day 42 started off with me being hella confused.

Daddy was home and recovery was going fine, but I was stuck on Bill's grand gesture at the hospital. I suppose a gift basket and flowers isn't really a grand gesture for someone with his wealth but that's not the point. The point is that he sort of...encroached on something that he hadn't been invited to.

My family can never, ever know about what I'm doing and Bill inserting himself the way he did had me on edge. And the confusing part was that I wasn't sure if I was wrong for feeling that way.

I got home from my shift at 9:30 that evening and I didn't come empty handed. Farrah said she'd been craving a Port and fries so I delivered it to her as soon as I walked in the door. We sat on the couch and I told her everything.

She chewed rapidly, a look of bliss covering her face. "I don't care if I beg you. Do *not* bring me another Port burger for the rest of the month. I'm trying to get in shape and this is not helping me."

"I won't. I promise." She was always complaining about being skinny-fat.

"Good. Now with that out of the way, I'm gonna be straight up with you. I know you don't wanna hear this but here it goes: you still have trust issues."

"No shit, bitch."

She laughed for awhile before composing herself. "I understand not wanting your people to know about him but in a normal situation, sending flowers would be a thoughtful gesture from a friend."

"I know. That's what's messing me up. Why did I have such a strong reaction?"

"You know why."

I did, but I was still having trouble acknowledging it. "When am I gonna be over it?"

Farrah set her burger on its greasy foil wrapper and wiped her fingers on a napkin. She grabbed my hand and looked in my eyes. "You don't just get over something like that. It's gonna take some time."

I nodded and tried not to cry. "Every time I think I'm getting better, something happens to remind me."

"Mani, it won't last forever. Eric is in jail and you have your whole life ahead of you. Just take it one day at a time, but don't let him rob you of having normal relationships with guys. Okay?"

Eric Duffy. My ex. The man who had isolated me from my friends and family, controlled me, and assaulted me in my parents' home. It was a lot to get over.

"Okay. So I don't say anything to Bill?"

Farrah shrugged. "I don't think you should say anything other than 'thank you.' He was just trying to be nice."

I knew she was right. There was some lingering sensitivity about men that I needed to deal with but I wasn't quite ready yet. Not all men are like Eric. Bill definitely wasn't, I could tell.

"I have news," she said, her eyes wide with excitement. "I have a sugar date!"

"Wait, what?"

"Mm hm. His name is Jacob and he's a trader."

"Did you do your research?"

"Of course. I found him on LinkedIn and he seems legit."

"Did you read the forums like I told you to?"

Farrah giggled. "Not yet."

"Farrah! Why--"

"I will, I promise."

"When's the date?"

"Two weeks."

I was about to lecture her when there was a knock at the door. "Are you expecting somebody?" I asked.

Farrah was already on her feet. "Something from Amazon."

She shuffled to the door and I sat back and closed my eyes. I was dozing off when I heard her say "Oh!"

I sat up and listened but I couldn't make out what she was saying. She returned about thirty seconds later with news. "Shawn's here to see you."

My heart pounded. What the hell was he doing here? And did I look good enough to see him? Wait, why would I even care about that if it's over?

I made my way to the door and there he was, looking sexy as always in a white V-neck t-shirt and dark blue jeans. "Why are you here?" I asked him.

"I wanted to apologize but you blocked me everywhere."

"And that wasn't a good enough hint?"

Shawn sighed and stared into my eyes. All I could think about was how juicy his lips were. He shook his head. "I'm sorry. I realize how that came off and I'm truly sorry."

I leaned against the door frame and gave my best blank stare. "Fine, I accept your apology."

A smile crept across those lips and I fought to avert my eyes. It was time for him to go. And yet...

"Listen," he said. "Is there any way I can see you again?"

"For what?"

He stepped closer and my body tensed involuntarily. "For this."

"What is this?" I asked through shallow breaths.

He took another step forward until he was close enough that I could feel his body heat. "So you gon' act brand new?"

I tried to speak but my breath caught in my throat. In all my years of dating, I had never felt chemistry this strong and this soon. It was disorienting. In lieu of speaking, I simply shook my head.

One more step and he would be close enough to

kiss me. One more step. I wanted it. I needed it. But it was bad for business. I tried to force myself to step backwards, to slam the door in his perfect face, but I was frozen.

"Yeah, I know," he said, seemingly reading my mind.

My entire body was tense, and goose bumps dotted my arms. I couldn't believe how out of control I felt. I took a deep breath and steadied myself. *Be strong. Be strong.* "Thank you for coming by. Take care," I said, only I didn't move an inch. All I had to do was back up and close the door but I couldn't.

And he took full advantage of my weakness.

He finally took that last step forward until he was directly in front of me. "You are so beautiful," he said as he leaned in. And that was it. I closed my eyes and received him, and his lips were as soft and full as they looked. They pressed against mine, gently at first, and then a little more firmly as his hand wrapped around my waist. And I don't know if he was pulling me or if my body did this on its own, but my pelvis tilted forward toward his. Any closer and there would have been dangerous contact.

We pulled away briefly but he immediately kissed me again, softly, gently, one time, then another, then again and again. Our lips were closed but somehow the kisses were more sensual than if we were full on French kissing. We kissed like lovers, like two people who had known each other longer than a week, like people who had already learned what the other liked. I almost...well, let's just say I pulled away quickly so as not to embarrass myself.

"So are you gonna unblock me, now?" he asked, grinning from ear to ear. Even in my flustered state I could see that he was feeling himself.

"Maybe."

"Oh, it's like that?"

"For now, yeah, it is."

Shawn put his hand on the back of my neck and squeezed gently as he spoke directly into my ear. "I want you to go in the house right now and un-block me. I'm gonna message you tonight. If I'm still blocked, I'll leave you alone. For good. If not, we'll go from there."

I nodded, and he kissed me again, a short peck on my cheek, before walking back to his car. I stood frozen as he drove away in that beautiful Porsche, my body on fire, my mind swimming in confusion.

I went back inside and fell onto the couch, still in a daze. Why was this such a struggle for me? I was supposed to be about my business, and Shawn had money and connections. He'd apologized and ex-plained and it should have been an easy, unemotional decision.

So why was I stuck?

Of all the corny, simplistic social media posts I've seen over the years, I've only saved two. The first one was cliché, but something I really needed to re-mind myself of after the disaster with Eric. It simply said: *You can't love anyone if you don't love yourself first.*

The second one really got me and was some-thing I wish I had known when I first started dating. It said: *If a man likes you, you'll know. If he doesn't, you'll be confused.*

I remember reading that and thinking ohhhh-hhh. Like the previous ten years of my life suddenly made perfect sense. And here I was, sitting on my couch, thinking about that post again. Only it didn't apply to my situation. Not at face value. It was actually the reverse. With Bill, everything was crystal clear. I was in it for the money.

But Shawn?

I was all discombobulated and kept losing sight of my goal. And the worst part is I couldn't tell if he was doing it on purpose or if he was affecting me by accident.

"Farrah!" I yelled. "I need you!"

I heard her grunt and then the shuffle of her house shoes on the carpet. She entered looking bleary-eyed and grumpy, her bonnet cocked to the side of her head. I'm sure she was sick of me.

"You fell asleep that fast?"

She gave me the most sarcastic glare ever. "It was a big burger. You know itis sets in quick."

I laughed. "Sorry. I need help with something."

She plopped next to me and sighed. "I'm listening."

I filled her in, and I spared no details. She actually stopped me at one point so that she could go into the kitchen and get a snack. I'm glad one of us was entertained by my messy life.

"So what should I do?" I asked.

She sat for a moment, chewing her chocolate

chip cookies. "Here's something I think you haven't realized yet. Those things you're experiencing? The rollercoaster of excitement and confusion? Those are called feelings. And you have them for Shawn."

Well, shit. "I don't even know him."

"You don't have to know somebody to feel things, even if the feeling is lust."

"Farrah, you don't understand. I mean...you saw him, right? He's fine as hell."

She nodded so hard it looked like it hurt.

"He's sexy, and he's rich, and he was my knight, and I wanna sit on his face. It's clouding my judgment!"

"What's wrong with sitting on his face?"

I gave her a blank stare.

"What? I think that's a valid question."

"You're not helping. I have a goal. I need to pay my tuition. I can't get sucked into a relationship or situationship or whatever else. I'm only doing this for the money."

"Mani, I love you. I really do. But if you can't handle everything that comes with your new...profession, then maybe you shouldn't be doing it. Either that, or just let white boy be your client and let Shawn be your friend with benefits."

"Maybe."

"The most important thing, after your tuition of course, is that you do get to ride his face. I don't think you should deprive yourself of that opportunity."

"This is why I love you."

"I know."

I thought about it some more over dinner. I didn't want a friend with benefits. I wanted my tuition paid. And it was smarter to hedge my bets and have two clients at once than to sacrifice a potential payday for sex, no matter how good that sex might be. I decided to keep my eye on the ball. I was going to set clear boundaries for Shawn and that was the end of it. No problem.

I logged in and unblocked him. Game on.

17

Imani

Day 40 of my countdown began with a phone call from the Knight. He said he was taking his boat out and he wanted me to come since I love to fish.

I had forgotten I told that lie.

I spent an hour googling furiously and finally found a few YouTube tutorials. By the time I was done watching, I felt confident enough to pretend to be someone who fishes every so often and is a little rusty.

I donned a neon yellow bikini underneath a blue sundress, just in case he wanted to swim. I don't do lakes and ponds but I could at least show off my suit and get my feet wet. My hair was wild and free in a twistout and I packed a few extra elastic bands just in case I needed to put it in a bun. I wore mascara and lip-gloss and slathered my face in sunscreen. I was ready.

"You're not taking me to Lake Lanier, are you?" I asked in the car.

"Hell nah. It's cursed."

"Okay, good."

"I'm taking you to a private lake."

"Do you own it?"

"No, but I'm a member. I own a dock there."

Whatever that meant. I smiled and nodded along and hoped I didn't make a fool of myself by asking stupid questions.

It took us about forty minutes to get there and I was getting restless but as soon as we cleared a long swath of trees, the water suddenly appeared in front of me. It was beautiful.

Shawn helped me out of the car. He was looking scrumptious in white button down and blue shorts. His legs were so muscular and sexy. I tried not to stare.

The boat was...a boat. I didn't know enough about them to know what I was looking at but it seemed like it was nice. The top part had a white leather seating area and wood flooring. Shawn showed me the inside and I was surprised it was so spacious. It certainly didn't look that way from the outside.

"Take a look around. I need to talk to the captain for a second," he said.

I took the opportunity to be nosy, looking into every nook and cranny. There was a living area with a television, a sound system, a table and chairs, and a small bar. The bedroom was small but the full bed fit nicely.

Later, once we got out on the water, he mixed me a Cosmo and grabbed a beer for himself. It was peaceful out there, and I could see the appeal. We hadn't started fishing yet but the poles were all set up. Shawn seemed content to stare at the water and talk.

"Why luxury real estate?" he asked.

I stared off into the distance where the sky met the water. "The way I grew up."

"Oh yeah? And how is that?"

"A whole lot different from you," I said with a chuckle. "Probably the total opposite."

"What was that like?"

"A lot of meatless dinners, moving from apartment to apartment, lights cut off, water cut off. At one point we lived in an extended stay." It felt so strange having to explain poverty to another black person. "I never felt stable or secure until we got our house. I was in high school by then. But I never, ever forgot how it felt to live like that."

"And now you wanna sell to people who have the life you wish you had?"

"I guess so, Dr. Freud."

Shawn laughed. "I'm not trying to analyze you. And I'm sorry you had to live like that."

I shrugged. "It is what it is."

He looked at me and I wondered what he was thinking. Did he pity me?

"Have you ever thought about actually living that life?" he said.

"Of course. And I will. I'm claiming that."

"Claiming it? What does that even mean?"

"You didn't grow up in the church?"

"Yeah. Episcopalian."

"Well I was Baptist and we were told to name it

and claim it and the Lord would provide it."

Shawn furrowed his brow. "I was taught if you don't work, you don't eat."

"My parents worked, Shawn."

"I'm not judging. I just don't understand it as a concept, that's all."

I was getting annoyed. "Anyway, I figure my career will put me in the right circles and then I can have the life I want."

We didn't speak for a few minutes. Shawn looked at me and asked, "can I give you some advice?"

I shrugged.

"You need to already be in the right circles to be successful in the field you're getting into."

"How would I go about doing that?"

"You could ask a friend. I'm sure there's a handsome, well-connected man out there somewhere who would love to help you."

I smiled at him and batted my eyelashes. "Your turn."

"My turn for what?"

"Tell me about you."

"Well--"

"I'm sorry, I've been dying to ask this. How did your family get so rich?"

He laughed. "Somebody way back in my family tree was a free person living in the north. They owned land there and eventually the government bought that land. My family took that money, moved back south, and started investing in other real estate and here we are."

"That's fascinating. So you were able to go all the way back in your family tree? I've always wanted to do that."

"Yeah, it's easier to do if there's a free person who kept good records. My granddaddy paid a genealogy expert for the legwork. My parents had the finished tree bound and gave all the kids their own copy."

My face lit up. "I would love something like that. You can pass it down to your children and their children and so on. Priceless."

"Yeah. If I have any."

"You don't want--"

"I don't know yet."

I shook my head and sipped my drink. It was getting me nice and loose. "Men are lucky. No biological clocks ticking in your ear."

"No, but I have a crotchety old man yelling in mine."

I laughed and pouted at him. "Poor Shawn."

"I'm just saying. Shit gets old after a while."

"Well then let's not talk about that. Tell me something else interesting."

"Like what?"

"Like...what's your favorite movie?"

He paused and scratched his temple. "Uh...probably Goodfellas."

I looked at him and smiled. "What's your real favorite?"

"You a mind reader?"

I didn't answer.

"Okay. Alright. Don't tell nobody this, alright? It's...*Titanic*."

I tried, I really did, but the laughter burst out of me like a geyser. "I'm sorry, I'm not laughing at you."

"See this is why I don't tell people that shit."

"Nooo. I'm sorry. That's actually really sweet. I didn't take you for a romantic."

"It ain't even about the romance. I mean yeah, that part is cool, but look," he said as he sat up straight and his voice got louder. "You also have some very interesting elements in the plot. There's history, class conflict, technological hubris, and that white dude falling and hitting that propeller. Shit was mad entertaining."

I giggled. "So you didn't pay *any* attention to the love story?"

"I mean...I ain't say all that. I may have felt some type of way when homegirl let my man die because she ain't wanna share that headboard."

"I feel you. There was enough room on there."

Shawn threw his hands up. "That's what I'm saying!"

His outrage was cute. "I always thought Rose was stupid. What was the plan if Jack lived? Was she really gonna go from the finer things in life to living like a pauper?"

He shrugged. "They were in love, though. Whatever that means."

"No. She was dickmatized."

"You've never felt like that about somebody? Like you have to have them and you don't give a damn about anything else?"

I took a deep breath. "Yeah. And it was the worst relationship of my life."

"Oh. Look, we don't have to talk--"

"It's okay. To make a real long story short, my ex was good in the beginning but he ended up being abusive."

"I'm sorry."

I wanted to slap some sense into myself. I kept forgetting I was on a business appointment. He didn't wanna hear this. That would not be getting his money's worth.

I perked back up. "Anyway, my philosophy is that relationships are one part feelings and the other part logic. Too many of us get some good dick and forget to think."

"Men are the same, trust me. Except for the dick part. Well, for some men. You know what I mean."

I laughed. "I do. So have you ever been in that deep with somebody?"

He took a pull from his beer. "Not deep enough for me to freeze to death in the ocean, no. But I have loved a few. Thought I would marry one. Didn't work out."

I nodded. "And here we are."

"Here we are."

We stared at each other for a moment before I looked away. "Give me one confession."

"You my priest now?"

"Just one."

"About what?"

"Something juicy."

He grinned. "Alright. Uhhhh...okay. I had sex on this boat. In the bow. With other boats in the water."

My eyes widened at the scandalous nature of that confession. "People saw you?"

"I don't see how they could have missed it. And if they didn't see, they damn sure heard."

I admit it. I was turned on. "So you're a freak? Interesting."

"Why is that interesting?"

"No reason."

He stared at me. "Your turn. Same rules apply."

"This is kinda embarrassing," I said.

"That's the best kind."

"Okay." I covered my face with my hands. "I've never...come...from sex."

Shawn took his sunglasses off to frown at me. "Are you serious?"

"It's not unheard of. Not for women."

"That's too bad. Do you know why?"

I shrugged. "Just figured I'm one of those women."

He sat quietly and tapped his finger on the side of his beer bottle. "It could be a mental thing."

"Meaning?"

"In my experience, some women aren't in touch with the mental part of it. It feels good to them but they just can't get there. They don't understand that the brain is as much a sex organ as anything else."

I was intrigued. "How much experience are we talking about?"

He raised his eyebrows. "Enough to know I can remedy that. If you're interested."

"I'm not fucking you on this boat."

"I'm not asking you to."

"Good. Because--"

"But if you cuss like that again I might tell Captain Dean to turn this boat back around."

"Oh, you like that?"

He grinned at me and I stared at his lips, mesmerized and turned on. "I just might," he said. "It's sexy."

"Well, Mr. Jeter, I will consider your offer and get back to you shortly."

"I know you will."

He had me. Shit. Get your head back in the game!

"I have another confession," he said. "Mine's embarrassing too, so you ain't out there by yourself."

"I'm listening."

"I don't know how to swim."

"What? How do you own a boat and can't swim?"

"Usually I wear a life jacket but I didn't wanna look like an idiot with you here so I don't have it today."

"What if you fell in?"

"I wouldn't."

"Real talk, that's dangerous. All that money and you won't take swimming lessons?"

He looked hurt, like I was scolding him. "You can teach me."

"Um, what?"

"Give me swimming lessons. I'll pay you, of course. We can start today when we get back to the house."

"You serious?"

"Why not?"

Why not, indeed. I quoted him $200 an hour and he agreed immediately, which only served to let me know I lowballed it. Lesson learned.

<u>*18*</u>

Imani

We got back to the house around 5 and went straight to the backyard, which was absolutely gorgeous. Hydrangeas lined the are just outside the patio door and each walkway was flanked by red and white roses. To the left was a large seating area with a fire pit at the center. To the right was a kitchen outfitted with two grills, a bar, a popcorn machine, a cotton candy machine, a refrigerator, and a range. Unreal.

Straight ahead was the large swimming pool with an attached Jacuzzi. Those were standard as far as pools go but the giant waterfall and double sided waterslide were not. Best of all, there were these steps going across the middle of the pool. They seemed to be floating on the water. I can't lie, I was impressed.

On the other side of the pool was a large, cherry wood bed with a canopy, complete with its own ceiling fan and lights. I'd never seen anything like this in real life, and I was glad I beat Shawn out here. I wanted to get all of my gawking out of the way before he could see.

I sat back on one of the chairs next to the pool and untied my robe to reveal my neon yellow bikini. Nothing looks better on brown skin than yellow, and I wanted all of Shawn's attention. The sun beamed down, scorching my skin and drawing out little beads of sweat all over, giving me the perfect glow. I hoped I looked like one of those rotisserie chickens you pass by in the deli, rotating and glistening and browning in the oven making your mouth water.

I heard footsteps but I held my pose. My eyes were open behind my mirrored sunglasses but he didn't know that. He stood over me and his eyes roamed every inch of me from head to toe. Finally, he shook his head ever so slightly which has only ever meant one thing: DAMN.

"I got our towels," he said.

"Oh! Thank you," I said like I didn't know he had been standing there. "You ready to get started?"

He sat on the chair next to me. "You want a drink first?"

I took my sunglasses off and smiled. "You trying to get me drunk before I get in the pool? I think that's how most Dateline episodes start off."

He chuckled. "I'm ready when you are."

I stood and walked over to the pool, hoping he enjoyed the view from behind. I jumped right in, never having been one to tip toe into the water. I love the shock of the cold. It's invigorating.

Shawn didn't move from the chair. "What's

wrong?" I asked him.

"Nothing. Just working up the nerve."

"Shawn, it's okay. Surely you've been in your own pool before."

He looked away and my mouth dropped open. "You've never been in your own pool?"

"Does the hot tub count?"

"No, it does not. Listen, if you're not ready, we don't have to do this."

"Nah, I already paid for the lesson," he said, punctuating it with a chuckle. "Just give me a second."

I could tell he was embarrassed but I found his fear endearing. "Okay. But just so you know, I'm standing right now. Where I am is about 5 feet so you can just walk right in."

I ducked under the water and swam leisurely. It was actually quite nice, temperature-wise, so there must have been some kind of temperature regulator. I resurfaced and floated on my back, staring up into the sky. Besides a few stray white wisps, it was a brilliant, clear blue heaven up there. I'm amazed people live like this every day. I'd only lived like this a few times in my life, on vacations to the Panama City and Hilton Head, and of course, Jamaica. I felt blessed and peaceful, and I prayed I would be able to live like this every day. Maybe one day.

"Show off," Shawn said behind me. I put my feet below me and turned to face him. "Look at you! How does it feel?"

He shrugged. "I'm straight. So tell me what to do."

I tried to sound professional. The man had paid me, after all. $200. We both knew I had no experience with this but that wasn't the point. "The first thing you need to understand is that your body will naturally float. Like if you laid down in the pool and did nothing, you wouldn't sink. People sink because they panic."

"Yeah but what do I *do*?"

"Look Mr. Billionaire. This isn't the boardroom. *I'm* in charge here, okay?"

He smiled. "Yes ma'am."

"So the first thing I want you to do is hold your breath and duck under water."

Shawn looked at the water, then back at me, and then at the water again. "Is that how you learned?"

"No, I learned when my cousins threw me into the pool without my floaties on. But obviously that was traumatic and wrong so we're not doing that. Just trust me. Okay?"

"Okay. How do I hold my breath? Do I hold my nose, or..."

"Are you serious? Just go under and don't breathe."

"Shit. Alright, check me out."

He did it. I was surprised but I think he really just didn't want me to see him as weak. When he came back up, I clapped for him. "You did it. Great job."

"Alright, what next?"

"Duck under, lift your feet, and relax your body completely. I just want you to see how it feels to have buoyancy."

"Look at you with the technical terms and shit."

"Shut up. Do what I said and then come up when you need more air."

To my surprise, again, he did it. Never underestimate the power and courage of a man with a big ego.

He stayed under for about 30 seconds and came back up. He wiped the water down his eyes and gasped for breath. "Very good," I said, and he shook his head.

"That's it?" he said.

"What?"

"I almost died down there and all I get is 'very good'?"

I shrugged.

"I'mma need some more encouragement from you. This is some scary shit I'm doing right now."

"What kind of encouragement?" I asked, knowing full well what he meant. See, this is how I get myself into trouble.

He grinned like a Cheshire cat and put his hand on his goatee. "Whenever I do something right, I get a kiss."

I frowned at him. "First of all, that's very seventh grade. And second of all, it wouldn't be professional."

Shawn laughed and came a little closer. "You're a trip. You like to play hardball, I see. Alright, what if I up your fee to $250 an hour."

I pretended to think about it, and was glad he wasn't aware that I would have done it for free. "I can agree to that."

"Cool. What's next."

"This time go under, float, and then open your eyes."

"Hold up...what does opening my eyes have to do with swimming?"

"I don't know, Shawn. What does opening your eyes has to do with driving? You need to know your surroundings and see where you're going. It doesn't hurt, I promise."

"This better be a damn good kiss."

I winked and he went under. I was so excited at the prospect of that kiss I didn't even look to see if he was following instructions. He resurfaced shortly after, wiping his eyes furiously. "You said it wouldn't hurt. It stings."

"Okay hold on, let me get you a towel." I swam over to the edge and grabbed a fluffy grey towel. When I got back over to him, his eyes were still closed. I gently dabbed his eyes and then the rest of his face and I could see him relax a little.

"Open for me," I instructed. "They're a little pink but that's normal. You'll get used to it." I continued to dab at his eyes like a loving girlfriend. Like he was mine. And he seemed to like that. He stared at me through heavy lidded eyes, first my lips, then my breasts. Even in the cool water, I could feel my body flushing with heat. When I turned to put the towel back, he grabbed my arm and gently pulled me back toward him. He leaned in and our eyes met first, then our lips. I dropped the poor towel into the water.

Our lips parted and our tongues met, gently caressed each other, exploring, seeing what was what. He wrapped his strong arms around my waist and I wrapped mine around his neck. I relaxed into him and his hands drifted lower to cup my ass. He squeezed and kneaded and our kiss got more aggressive. We were hungry for each other, that much was clear. And when I moved in closer, I felt his erection on my stomach and it jolted me back to reality.

I pulled away and smiled. "Okay, so good job on opening your eyes."

"Imani..."

Be strong. "The next thing I want you to do--"

"Imani!"

"Yes?"

"Come here," he said, his voice low and deep.

"We need to finish the lesson," I said weakly, my resolve crumbling to dust. I couldn't even look him in the face. The pull was too strong. I stared at the towel as it floated next to us and waited for the moment to pass. It didn't.

"Fuck the lesson," he said.

Indeed.

19

Imani

I give up.

I was too weak to fight it anymore. Just...whatever. I deserved this after what I'd been through. Maybe it didn't have to be complicated. Maybe we could have sex and then go back to our regular arrangement and nothing would have to change. That's what I told myself.

Shawn took my hand and led me up the pool steps. He grabbed a towel and dried me off, starting with my shoulders, then my back, and then my butt and thighs. Last, my feet. After he dried himself off, he led me down the walkway toward the canopy. A light breeze drifted through the cream curtains, and they appeared to be beckoning us over. He positioned me in front of the bed and stood in front of me. His chest was a mound of muscle and his abs were cut up. I couldn't believe this man was almost 40.

He grabbed my face and kissed me softly, and then his hands drifted down to my sides to my hips, where he grabbed the strings from on my bikini bottoms. He stared into my eyes as he slowly pulled the strings. Once they were loose, he hooked his finger down the front of the bottom and pulled it down.

"Shawn--"

"Shhhhhh," he said, putting a finger to my lips.

Okay.

He sat me down and knelt in front of me. I knew what was coming but when he pushed my legs apart, I gasped in surprise. And partly in anticipation. It had been so long.

He kissed his way up my thighs, his hands gripping my hips, and I throbbed in anticipation. He lingered at my inner thighs, kissing softly, lightly nipping my skin with his teeth, teasing me. I couldn't stand it anymore so I moved to scoot closer to his face. He slapped my hip and hummed "mm mm," a subtle rebuke that let me know he was in control. And so I settled in and waited for the pleasure. It was right there, but he was going at his own pace.

"Shawwwwwn," I whined, and he squeezed my hips tighter. "Please," I said, and thankfully, he finally kissed his way up to my center and kissed those lips as passionately as he had kissed me earlier. His tongue vigorously worked its way up, down, in, and out, driving me to wrap my legs around his neck and arch my back. My body shuddered as the exquisite pressure began to build. I moaned quietly, biting my lip to keep from yelling out. I was almost there when he paused.

My eyes flew open. "Nooo, I was close!" I

whined.

"Stop holding back," he said. "Nobody can hear you out here."

Bet.

And then he resumed giving me the best head of my life. I did what he asked; I let go and loudly expressed my enjoyment. The more vocal I was, the more voraciously he fed on me. The pressure began to build again and I gripped his forearms, digging my nails into his warm flesh. He responded by sealing his lips on my clit and sucking gently. My climax came swiftly and intensely, and Shawn was so turned on he moaned along with me.

Afterward, as I lay there staring at the sky, with nature all around me, and aftershocks rippling through my body, I panted and fought to catch my breath. I felt like I was on top of the world, and I relished that feeling for a while until another feeling crept in. Worry. What was gonna happen next?

In an ordinary situation, we would have sex. Good sex, if the previous ten minutes were anything to go by. But nothing about this situation was ordinary.

And then there was the money issue. Was I supposed to ask for extra for allowing him to go down on me? Or was it better to let it slide and pretend it was part of the lesson? It was all so confusing.

The bed shifted beside me and I looked to my left to see Shawn lying next to me. His print was conspicuous, straining hard against his swim trunks.

Be strong.

I flashed a smile and placed my hand on his bare chest. "That was good."

He smiled back. "Oh, I know."

I giggled and rolled my eyes. "So cocky."

"For good reason. That was the best you ever had, admit it."

It was, but I wouldn't. "It was up there."

Shawn turned toward me and propped himself up on his elbow so that he was looking down at me. "That's not the only thing I'm good at."

I believed him. I believed the hell out of him. But I needed to keep my wits about me. I was beginning to feel powerless. I needed to get out of here. Now. "I believe you," I said, and immediately regretted it.

He leaned down and kissed me and I wanted to reach down and touch it. It was right there, just a few inches away. Just one touch, one caress, and that would be enough.

I wrapped my arm around his neck and moved my right hand toward his trunks. My eyes were closed and I landed on his abs. I inched my hand down, down, down, and then suddenly Shawn pulled away.

I opened my eyes. "What's wrong?"

"I'm kicking myself for this but I need to run back to the house and get some condoms."

Yes! Perfect opportunity for me to get the hell out of there. "Actually, it's getting late and I have a shift tonight."

Shawn opened his mouth to speak but then closed it abruptly. We stared at each other for several seconds and the heat between us was insane. And then I realized I was still naked below the waist. I sat up and reached down to pick my bottoms off the grass. Shawn watched be as I stepped into them and pulled them up. As I tied the strings on the right, he tied the strings on the left. With every brush of his fingers on my skin, little shocks of electricity crackled through my body.

I wanted him so bad.

We walked back to the pool and I collected the towels. He watched me in amusement before speaking. "You can leave those. My cleaning lady will get them."

"It's a habit. I don't mind."

"I mind. I don't want you working when you're here. At least not that kind of work."

Why? Why was he tempting me?

We made our way back into the house and I chalked day 40 up as a W. I got mine, got $500, I didn't do something stupid, and I left him wanting more. Not a bad day's work.

20

Imani

Three days later, we gathered at Port for Arianna's baby shower. And by "we," I mean the employees, Fran's family, and a few of Arianna's teenage friends. It was a very odd assortment of people but then again, baby showers for teenagers are odd events.

I'd known Arianna since she was a pink-cheeked ten-year-old with braces. Now she was a grown woman, or as close to grown as a girl gets without actually being an adult. She was still a tiny little thing, only she now had a protruding belly.

Fran said the father was some tatted up, jobless loser in Arianna's class, which--aren't they always? But Fran was making the most of it like any mother who loves her daughter in spite of her mistakes. She had transformed the back room of her dive bar into a beautiful, pink tulle-filled wonderland with balloons and flowers and little cakes shaped like baby butts. The pink was an odd choice since Arianna wanted to be surprised by the gender. I guess it was wishful thinking on Fran's part.

Since I had a little extra change in my pocket, I didn't have to embarrass myself by showing up empty-handed. I always stick to the registry because I have no imagination, and today was no different. I spent $29.88 on a bottle warmer, including gift wrapping since I suck at that, too.

"Hey, pretty girl," Fran said as she approached my table. "Let's move to the back. I don't feel like listening to a bunch of squealing teenage girls."

I grabbed my plate and walked to the back booth, thinking about Shawn the whole time. His smile. His laugh. His face between my thighs...

I joined Fran and Taya, another waitress, and tried to get Shawn out of my mind. "When are we playing the games," I asked.

Fran snorted. "Never. Who actually likes playing baby-shower games? It's such bullshit. I'm giving everyone a gift bag and calling it a day."

"I never thought about it but you're right. I hate them."

"Me too," Taya said. "And the chocolate in the diaper thing? That's disgusting."

Fran took a swig of beer. "Thank you. And listen, she's lucky we even had a fucking shower. I had half a mind to just buy everything myself. The last thing I wanted to do was celebrate this clusterfuck."

"Yeah but all babies deserve to be celebrated," I said between bites of my slider. "You'll be glad you did it."

Taya nodded. "For real. If you didn't you'd probably look back and regret it."

Fran shrugged. "I told y'all. The guy is a fucking loser. I might be a little happier about this if she had picked somebody with a future and an ounce of sense in his head."

I snorted. "Like mother, like--"

"Don't say it!" she said to me. "I'll break this bottle over your head if you say it, Mani!"

"I'm just saying. Didn't you tell me you always liked bad boys?"

She gave me a blank stare before taking another swig. "Which is why I preached so hard against that. And then she went right on out and did the opposite."

"That sounds about right," Taya said. "You didn't do anything wrong. Kids do what they want."

Fran shook her head and blinked rapidly, tears pooling in the bottom of her eyes. "I just want her to be happy. And to make something of herself."

"She still wants to go to college, right?" I said.

"Yeah."

"Well there you go. It's doable."

Fran sniffed and sat up straight. "You're right. It'll be fine. Moms go to school all the time, right?"

"Half the women in my classes have kids," I said. "And a lot of times, they end up being the better students."

"Speaking of which...did you figure out your tuition deal?"

I glanced at Taya. I wanted to tell Fran anyway and she had just given me my opening. But I didn't want anyone else to know. "Not yet. I'm weighing some options."

We ate in silence until Taya stood up. "I'm going to get another plate." I moved aside so she could get out and then plopped back down.

I took a deep breath. "Okay, I've been...dating."

"Good for you!"

"I have two potentials right now. They've already given me a little bit. If I play things right, I should have enough to pay by the deadline."

Fran smiled brighter than she had all day. "I knew you'd be good at it. If I had your youth and body, I'd be doing it too. Still."

"Wait, what? What do you mean 'still'?"

Fran shrugged and tilted her head. "I was a hot little number back in my day. There were some gentlemen who were very good to me financially. We didn't have a website or anything but we made it work. How do you think a country girl like me owns this big city bar?"

I could see that. I put my palm in the air and high-fived her. "Why'd you stop?"

"I wanted a *family*," she said, like it was a dirty word. "I was too young and dumb to realize I didn't actually need one. But I got my babies out of it. I just wish I had kept one foot in the game though. Just one. The profit potential is infinite."

I thought for a moment. "And how would you do that?"

"Are you kidding? College girls like you are a rich old man's dream. I could have made a killing making my own real-life version of those websites you read for pointers. Get it going like a pyramid. Plus, there's safety in numbers. Nobody out there doing it on their own without anyone to talk to."

"Yeah, it sucks not having anybody who really gets it."

One of Arianna's friends walked over to our table. "She's ready to do the cake."

"Of course she is," Fran said as she eased out of the booth.

As I watched them walk away, I tried to picture Fran as a Madame and the visual made me chuckle. She probably would have been good at it, too. She was organized and laser focused. Kinda like me.

21

Shawn

I can't stop thinking about Imani.

I thought about her while I was flossing my teeth, and then I got hard. Gerald brought me a Bojangles chicken biscuit, my favorite, and then I thought about her and got hard. Nita gave me some bad news at the office--we were outbid on an important property--and while I was sitting there pissed off, I thought about her and got hard.

Do you see my dilemma?

I thought I was doing the right thing the other day when I went down on her. That whole not coming from sex thing was really weighing on me. I wanted to fuck, don't get me wrong, but I didn't want her to think it was a demand or expectation. I don't mind taking things slow. But of course I went down on her and got hard, and it's been rough ever since.

I had to put that shit out of my mind, though. I had more pressing things to concern myself. Namely the meeting Pop called to discuss some family business. Because in our family, business was always at the center of everything. I don't mind it. It's the reason I can live the way I do. It would just be nice if sometimes we could get together and just be...us.

I was gathering my shit to leave when I she popped into my head again. That day...by the pool...her body...her moans...I enjoyed that more than I've enjoyed full-on sex with other women.

Get your head in the game, boy. That's what I tell myself when it's time to focus. And I needed to be on today.

I made my way to the first floor conference room with Nita on my heels. I arrived before DJ, but Pop and my uncle Randall were already seated. Randall rose to greet me with a hearty, "good to see you, young man!" and a warm hug. Pop nodded in my direction.

"Where's DJ?" I asked. Nita set a cup of coffee in front of me and took her seat to my left. "He's not late yet. I'm just wondering."

"Call him and see," Pop said.

Randall loosened his tie and leaned back. "He better get here soon. I got somewhere to be."

This is what frustrates me about my brother. He wants the big job, and he deserves it in my opinion, but he doesn't give so much as an inch extra to the company. He's in the door by 9 or so and he's out promptly at 5. He treats it like a corporate job rather than a legacy. I guess I understand it; his wife and kids want him home. But that's the paradox of this particular issue. The very thing Pop demands in exchange for his approval is the thing that prevents total commitment to the job.

I checked my phone. Imani hadn't called or texted me but that wasn't a surprise. I liked that she wasn't all up under me all the time. Mystery is an art, and it's rare for a woman her age to have mastered it.

"I'm here, let's get to work," DJ announced as he walked in the door. Jermaine, his admin, was close behind him. My sister-in-law was the impetus behind that hire; she was dead set against her husband having a female subordinate. Randall greeted him with a hug just as he had me, and Pop nodded again.

DJ patted my back as he passed me and sat to my left. "What's good, little brother?"

I flashed him a genuine smile. "Just you, play-boy."

"Alright, enough of that," Pop grouched. "We have some pressing business. First, the Alpharetta space. Randy, what do you know?"

Randall slid a stack of clear folders toward the middle of the conference table. "Here's Mark's write-up. He thinks it's fairly straightforward but he wants us to talk to the bank before he gives a final recommendation."

We had our eye on an office complex in Alpharetta. It sat in a growing community that was beginning to skew younger and our plan was to transform the complex into a hipster-friendly coworking and retail space. I'm talking a fully-stocked coffee bar that converts to a real bar for happy hour, a library, a lounge with video games, a computer lab, classrooms, and a small gym. It was the most ambitious and progressive project we'd ever started.

Pop turned to me. "Did you speak to Ms. Porter?"

"Yeah, she said our credit and cash reserves are fine and she sees no impediment to us acquiring the loan."

"Good. Good," Pop said. He turned his attention to DJ next. "What did Al say?"

Al Ross, our accountant, wasn't Pop's favorite person. In fact, a few years ago, Pop announced he would not have any further contact with Al. Nobody knows why and nobody asked. Nobody asked Pop why he did much of anything. Pop answers to no one, and will shame you just for asking.

DJ cleared his throat. "Not yet."

"Excuse me?" Pop said, and the room was suddenly filled with tension.

"I got swamped this week, Pop. I did send him an email, though. He just never got back to me."

Pop glared through his glasses. "I'm not sure if you know this, but Al's office is one floor down." Sometimes it's hard to tell whether Pop is being sarcastic or if he truly believes you're as stupid as you sound.

DJ looked embarrassed. "I know that, Pop."

"Oh. Okay, good. Then I take it your failure to complete this simple task was due to an oversight and not wanton stupidity."

The room was completely silent, everyone too tense to speak and too shook to move. Pop was like a rattlesnake. When he got going, it was best to stay perfectly still so that he didn't set his sights on you.

Finally, he took his glasses off and rubbed his eyes. "I can't do this by myself, y'all. This particular endeavor is more complex than our usual so I need us to have our ducks in a row."

DJ fiddled with his necktie. "Pop, I apologize."

Pop peered at my brother over his glasses. "Thank you. That's money in the bank."

My brother stared down at the table at the sarcastic rebuke. I hated to see this, I really did, but I knew better than to get between them. It didn't seem fair. My brother had saved me from countless ass-whoopins over the years at the hands of boys that were bigger and stronger than me. Many of the lumps he's taken, at home and otherwise, were meant for me.

I studied my big brother. He'd gained a lot of weight over the years and his hairline was running for its life but we still have the same face.

"This will likely be my last acquisition before I get out of here and it has to be right. Do y'all understand?" Pop said.

Randall nodded. "We got you, Dennis."

"I think you all know this whole thing is completely out of my comfort zone. But Shawn believes in this and I trust him. Just don't make me out to be a fool."

"We got you, Pop," I said, echoing my uncle.

"It would be a wonderful turn of events if everyone shared your opinion and commitment."

I glanced at DJ, trying to catch his eye and commiserate but he continued to stare at the table and fiddle with his tie. Finally, he said, "I'm all in, Pop. I promise. No more mistakes."

That seemed to pacify him and I was relieved. The last time we'd had a family meeting, DJ and Pop almost came to blows. I don't even remember what the argument was about. I just remember getting the distinct impression that the disagreement was about something else entirely. But I'm not the type to play detective. Do what you want as long as you ain't messing with my money or my girl.

DJ cleared his throat. "Pop, Uncle Randall, I'm glad we met today because I wanted a chance to talk to you about my future here."

Randall frowned. "Shawn, do you mind stepping out?"

"It's cool, Uncle. He can stay. It concerns him, too."

Aw, shit. What the hell was he up to?

"Have you all given any more thought to the future of this company? Leadership-wise?"

Pop and Randall exchanged a look. "Well," Pop said as he removed his glasses, "that decision has been made. And if I recall correctly, you were there when we made it."

Fuck. I should have left when I had the chance.

DJ soldiered on. "I remember that conversation. I guess I was just wondering if--"

"If we changed our minds?" Pop said. "We didn't. Anything else?"

DJ sat back and chuckled. "Can I at least get a

reason?"

Against my better judgment, and based purely on emotion, I spoke up. "I agree with DJ. I think you all owe him a reason."

Pop and Randall looked at each other again. Randall spoke this time. "This meeting is adjourned."

Pop left before we could say another word and Randall turned to me with anger in his eyes. "Stop pushing him. I'm warning you."

"Warning me?" I said. "What does that even mean? Warning me about what?"

"To leave him be. This is not your battle. Do your job and pull off this workspace deal. That's your task, hear?"

Randall hurried from the room and it was only my brother and I, plus Dita. We stared at each other until DJ gathered his stuff and walked quietly from the room.

Dita cleared her throat. "If I were you, I would listen to your uncle."

"Why?"

"If you keep going at your father, he's gonna let the truth come out, and that's no good for anyone."

"Wait, you know what this is about?"

"Leave it alone, Shawn. Trust me."

22

Imani

I sat in my hot-ass car and sweated my edges out. It was fine, though. I was just headed to see my daddy and he didn't care what I looked like.

It was shaping up to be a pretty good day. Traffic was light and the breeze blowing in through the windows was consistent. Beyoncé blasted through my speakers and I sang and danced along at various intervals.

I was feeling great.

So great, I decided to do something I hadn't done in a long time. The mall was on the way to my parents' house so I decided to stop in and buy myself a little something.

Shawn texted me this morning and it put a big smile on my face.

> **I've been thinking about you since our date. When are you free again?**

I hadn't answered yet because I wanted him to sweat a little bit. I wanted him to miss me. It was tak-ing everything in me not to dive into this thing headfirst, but I still had 36 days left and I was nowhere near my goal.

Nevertheless, it was time to treat myself with some of my hard-earned cash. I parked at Macy's and walked in slowly. I had missed that mall smell, the aroma of clean clothes, leather, perfume, and food. I breathed deeply and smiled. This was home.

The cosmetics section was straight ahead. I stopped by and looked through the glass case. I wasn't even sure what kinds of fragrances I liked. I had strictly been a Bath and Body Works kind of girl up to that point. I needed help.

I spotted a salesgirl and approached her. Her name was Dee. "Hi, I need help picking a perfume."

"I can help you with that! Is this for you or is it a gift for someone?"

"No, it's for me."

"What kind of notes do you like?"

"Notes?"

"Oh girl, come sit," she said, gesturing toward the stools in front of the fragrance counter. I took my seat and she walked back behind the counter. She produced several glossy 3x5 cards in different colors.

"Fragrance notes are sort of like the notes in music. Top notes, heart notes, and base notes." She pointed at each card, which were labeled with the notes and their corresponding smells. "When you smell a fragrance, you're looking for the three notes to be in harmony with one another. If you're turned off by the top note--the one you smell first--then you likely don't stick around for the other two. So let's get you some samples and see if anything grabs you."

Dee set about laying out the little paper arrow-looking things, spraying one and letting me sniff, then the next. She was efficient and passionate about her work, pointing out which ones were citrus-y, which ones were floral, which ones were musk-y, and so on. By the end, I had a slight headache.

She sold me on a small bottle of Moschino Toy 2--apparently I'm a citrus girl--and she threw her card in the bag for good measure.

"You have wonderful taste. Come back and see me so we can choose your next fragrance. A girl should have at least three good ones," she'd said with a smile.

When I got to the car, I opened the little teddy bear shaped bottle and gave myself a small mist of my new perfume. I sat for a moment breathing it in and smiled at my good fortune. If things kept going the way they had been, she would definitely be seeing me again.

Giovanni let me in the house and he didn't look happy. In fact, he opened the door and immediately turned and walked upstairs as if I wasn't even there. I told y'all he wasn't my favorite, and stuff like this is why. I try to be understanding. After all, I was a moody teenager once. But sometimes his behavior bordered on disrespect, and that's something I just do not care for.

My mother was in the kitchen when I walked in. "Hi Mama," I said as I grabbed her in a hug.

"Hey sweetie. Ooh, what is that?"

"What?"

"What you're wearing. It smells so good."

I smiled. "Oh, it's perfume. I just got it."

"What's it called."

"Moschino is the brand. The name is Toy 2."

"Oh, I've heard of Moschino. Isn't it expensive?"

I grabbed a banana from the fruit bowl and peeled it open. "Um, I don't think so. It was a really small bottle."

My mother eyed me quizzically and I stood there and let her analyze me. I couldn't say for sure but it felt like she was calculating the dollars in her head. "So how's Daddy?" I asked.

"About the same." Mama lowered her voice and moved closer to me. "Mani, he's got me worried."

My stomach dropped. "What is it?"

"Well his knee is fine. It's healing the way it's supposed to. I have a chart and pictures and so far, so good with that."

I breathed a sigh of relief and leaned back against the counter. "So what's the problem?"

"It's his mental state. I think he's...depressed." She spat the word out like it was bitter on her tongue. "I can't snap him out of it."

"What's he depressed about?"

"He won't say. He won't even admit that he's different. He just tells me I worry too much. But I...look, just go see for yourself. I'm done for the day, I can't deal with it anymore."

"Okay. Go lay down or something. I'll take care

of Daddy." It was the least I could do.

"I can't lay down. I have to cook dinner."

"I got it, Mama." I looked at my phone to check the time. "I don't have to be at work for another couple of hours. I'll throw something together for you. Just go relax."

Mama didn't speak. She simply smiled and put her hand on my cheek. I knew that to be a 'thank you.'

I took a deep breath and steeled myself, concerned about what I would find in that back bedroom. I crept down the hall and heard the tv. Judge Joe Brown, his favorite. He couldn't have been too far gone, then.

"Daddy?" I asked, poking my head in.

He was sitting up in bed with his leg propped on a pillow. He looked a little pale and a shade thinner but other than that, nothing seemed wrong. "Hey princess. Come on in here."

I gave him a careful hug. "You look good. How do you feel?"

"Eh."

"Eh?"

"Pain's not bad but I'm just not myself right now." His pajamas were dirty and his hair was overgrown. His fingernails jutted from his fingertips, misshapen and jagged. It was unnerving.

"Is that what's bothering you?" I said.

"Who said anything is bothering me?"

"Nobody, I just--"

"Your mama told you that? Don't listen to her."

"But Daddy--"

"I mean it! That woman is sick of waiting on me, that's all." He sighed and shook his head. "And I can't blame her."

"She's just worried about you."

"Hell, I'm worried about me too. Mani, I'm a grown man. I like to do for myself. And for other people. I'm not comfortable being fussed over and waited on."

We watched Judge Joe Brown snap on people until the commercial break. As an ad for Pine Sol played in the background, I turned to my daddy and grabbed his hand. "What do you want? Do you want Mama to stop bringing you food and helping you in and out of bed?"

"I want...," he began, his head dropping low. "I wanna be my old self again. I wanna mow the lawn and work on your car and play basketball with the boys. And take your mama dancing like we used to. That's not asking much, right?"

"It's not too much and maybe you'll be able to do some of those things again. I don't know about basketball but the other stuff isn't too strenuous. Right?"

He said nothing.

"What can I do?" I asked, hopeful that he would ask for a hug or a kiss from the princess. Instead, he glared at me.

"Nothing. Ain't nothing anybody can do. I just want all y'all to leave me be." He was quiet for a moment before saying, "and you've done enough."

Tears welled up in my eyes but I left the room before he could see.

My mother was waiting in the living room when I came out. She had a mug of coffee and a magazine in her hand. "Well?"

I shook my head. "He's really down. I've never seen him like this."

Mama sighed and tossed her magazine on the table. "I'm at my wits' end."

"He said he wants to be left alone."

"I'm sure he does but he's gotta work on his recovery. He can't just lay around. And guess who's gotta be there to make him do it?"

"Are the boys helping?"

"On the weekends. They have too much to do during the week."

"I'm sorry. I'll try to come out here more often."

"That would be nice."

She didn't say it but I know she was dying to. I figured I'd go ahead and relieve the tension right then. "He still blames me, doesn't he?"

Mama stared out the window instead of at me. "I don't know."

I didn't believe her. "He does. And so do you. Right?"

Mama set her mug on the coffee table and rubbed her eyes. "I don't blame you. I do think your poor choices are what got us here."

Even though I knew it was coming, it still stung. Because she was right.

Everyone told me not to date Eric Duffy. I met him when I was 19, and for two years, he controlled every aspect of my life. He was older (30) and I was young and inexperienced and he took advantage of that. It got to the point where I was dependent on him for everything, including my tuition for school. The culmination of that toxic relationship was him holding me hostage at my parents' house. My dad came home and got the gun away from him while I called the police but Eric fought back and injured him. Daddy's wrist healed quickly but the knee...

I had plenty of warning, and I ignored plenty of red flags. My parents had every right to blame me. But that didn't make it any easier.

"What are you cooking?" Mama said, as if she hadn't just ethered my soul.

I sniffed and steeled myself. "How does spaghetti sound?"

After dinner, I said my goodbyes and went to my car, still feeling down about the day. Seeing my daddy still suffering for my mistakes made me long for the day I could take care of them. I was just a year away from that if I could just keep my head on straight.

I checked my phone and saw that Bill had texted me.

> *Hi there, bad news. Got called away on business.*
> *Will be in NYC until Sunday. Rain check?*

Nooooooo! I really needed that money. I responded:

> *Of course. Enjoy your trip. Can't wait*
> *to meet up when you return.*

This was a wrench. A huge, annoying wrench

in my plan. But little did I know, it was about to get worse. I was just turning the corner out of my parents' subdivision when my car began to sputter. I heard a few bangs and a pop and then it took its last breath and died.

23

Day 36 continued to get shittier. My little Civic was dead, or at least very, very ill, and I had a shift at work that I absolutely could not miss.

If Daddy were healthy, he would have raced outside and gone to work on my car, having me up and running in plenty of time. If not, he would have just driven me himself. But Daddy is down for the count and his truck is a stick shift which prevented me from borrowing it. My mother needed her car to get to work. I was stuck.

The only other option was to Uber to work and back to my apartment after my shift but I didn't have the money for that. I still had cash from my dates with Shawn but in all likelihood, I would need to spend all of it to fix my car.

I wonder what it must be like to not get set back by setbacks. To be flush with cash at all times and never have to agonize about whether or not you'll be able to fix the stuff that breaks. That's why I work so hard, so that I can one day feel at peace for an entire day without something lurking just around the bend.

I sighed in my hot car and pulled up the Uber app. Two steps forward, two steps back.

My shift was uneventful and I made it home in once piece, but when I sat down and counted out my money, I was reminded of how far I was from my goal. And that made me do something I had been fighting the urge to do: I messaged Shawn.

You were on my mind just now so I thought I'd say hi.

He responded four minutes later.
Hello to you, too. You been on my mind all day.

I'm not gonna lie. I smiled. I was happy he had been thinking about me. Not just because I needed money, but because I...missed him. Shit.

Me: How was your day?

Shawn: Long and tedious. When can I see you?

Got him. We set a date for the next day. I told him to surprise me.

He picked me up promptly at 7:30. He told me to dress casual so I wore some grey Fashion Nova high waist jeggings that hugged every curve and a pale pink crop tee that showed the tiniest bit of midriff. One day...one day soon...I would buy jeans that were thicker than a piece of notebook paper.

But I could see in his eyes, and his stare, that he appreciated the outfit, cheap as it was. He looked sexy in blue jeans, a beige v neck, and some shoes I didn't recognize that looked hella expensive.

He greeted me with a soft kiss on the lips. "You look good as hell."

I looked him up and down. "Thank you. So do you."

"I'm just trying to impress you, you know that."

He didn't have to try hard. "The effort is appreciated. So where are you taking me?"

He laughed. "I wanna take you home with me if I'm being real."

And I wanted to go.

He continued. "I felt kinda bad that I took you to that gala for our first date. We're going to the club."

"You go to the club?" I asked. What I didn't say was 'at your age,' but I was damn sure thinking it. Not that he looked old, it's just...I couldn't picture him as the old nigga in the club.

"I go sometimes. I like to dance."

"Which club?"

"Synergy."

Holy shit. I'd never been but I'd definitely heard of it. Only high rollers were strolling up in there. It was where the ball players went on All-star weekend and where Jay Z and his ilk had their concert after parties. It's even been said that Obama rolled through once but that's an urban legend. Maybe I could get Shawn to tell me if that was true.

"Am I dressed okay for that?"

He looked me up and down, damn near drinking me with his eyes. "You could wear a Publix bag in there and you'd still be the baddest bitch in the room."

Well.

I smiled coquettishly and kissed him on the cheek. That was all he was gonna get for now, even though I wanted a hell of a lot more. I was *not* gonna get caught up tonight, not before a new arrangement had been made. Bill wasn't a sure thing anymore so I needed to do this right.

Gerald let us out at the curb and it was just like in the movies: The guy at the door waved us in after dapping Shawn up, and everyone who was standing in line was staring and wondering who the hell were we. And I liked it.

Trap music pounded through the speakers as we walked through the crowded club. It was a mixed crowd, mostly black but with a good number of white folks and a few Asians. I saw everything from suits and dresses to jeans and rompers. But everybody had one thing in common: they looked rich.

Shawn grabbed my hand and led me through a congested spot. Once we were through, I found myself in an area with a leather couch and a table of liquor in front of us.

VIP, bitches!

We sat and Shawn whispered something in the hostesses' ear. She nodded and handed me a menu and a key fob with a little green button on it. "I'm Angelina and I'll be serving you this evening," she shouted into my ear. "If you need food, a drink, the restroom, or anything else, just press this button, okay love?"

"Okay, thank you!" I shouted back, and she disappeared into the crowd. The same crowd I've stood in before. That congested spot in front of us was filled with wannabes and interlopers hoping to get chose. And here I was, already chosen. Damn, it was a rush.

Shawn was busy shaking hands and talking people up so I stared at the menu and wondered what I would eat first. The choices were lobster tail filled with caviar, oysters in vodka sauce, truffle fries with fresh garlic and parmesan, Portobello mushroom and bacon pizza, venison sliders, grass-fed beef patties, and crab lasagna bites. And at the bottom of the menu, it stated, *personal chef open to requests*.

I turned it over and saw VIP printed conspicuously on the back. Everybody else in the house who was eating had chicken wings on their plates. I was a little overwhelmed but finally settled on the lobster tail and fries. I pressed the little green button and felt a weird surge of empowerment, and when I saw Angelina rushing toward me, I sat up a little straighter. This was the life.

After she left, Shawn approached the table with two other men, both fine like him. "Imani, I want you to meet a couple of people. This tall, ugly nigga is Trenton Devore. He works in acquisitions at Northstar."

"Nice to meet you," I said sweetly as we shook hands.

"And this dude ain't shit but you should know him because he's in your field. This is Aaron Huntley. He's at Berkshire Hathaway."

That was a name I definitely knew. Berkshire Hathaway, not Aaron. "Nice to meet you, Aaron."

We shook and he handed me his card. "Shawn said you're looking to get into luxury?"

"Yes."

"Hit me up if you need anything."

"Thank you so much!" I said, feeling overwhelmed again. Was this really my life? Was I in the VIP making connections with people in my field and eating truffles and shit? Unbelievable.

I put the card in my purse and sat back, my head swimming. Shawn sat beside me and I leaned over and kissed him on the lips. "I'm having fun already," I purred.

"Good. That's all I want. I wanna see you happy and unbothered."

You and me both.

My food came so that was the end of our conversation for the moment. I went in on them truffle fries and the caviar was weird but good. Angelina came and mixed a lemon drop and Shawn had a couple of shots with Aaron and the other folks in the VIP next to ours. Once I finished my drink, I downed a shot of whatever Shawn had and my chest started burning. I was good and tipsy, something I shouldn't have been. I knew better. But I sauntered over to Shawn and put my arms around him from behind. He tensed for a second but when he looked back and saw me, he relaxed and put his hand over mine. It was...intimate.

"You good?" he yelled over his shoulder. I didn't

answer, I simply pulled him backwards and over to our section.

"I'm good. Let's dance," I said in his ear.

"Oh, word? You think you can hang with me?"

"We'll see."

I grabbed his hand and led him to the dance floor. I can't even tell you what song was playing, but the bass pounded and compelled my hips to move. Even through my vodka-soaked haze, I could see that Shawn had plenty of rhythm. His swag was off the charts as he caught my flow and moved with me. I turned around and twerked a little bit and he put his hands on my hips and watched me work. His grip was strong and dominant, the kind of aggression I like.

The dj switched to an afrobeats track and I started to wine as the beat moved through my soul and flowed out of my limbs. The multicolored lights bounced around the room and smoke rose from somewhere and made the room hazy. The atmosphere was sexy as hell and I was getting caught up.

Somewhere, in the back corner of my mind, a voice was telling me, "remember your goal. Get your money." But it was really quiet and easy to ignore. And so I did.

We made our way back to our section and sat on the couch, a lot closer this time. Shawn's breath was warm on my ear as he leaned over and spoke to me. "When I'mma get my next lesson? Tonight?"

"Are you serious? It's not exactly swimming weather out there."

"We could still do the lesson though. In the

shower."

"In the shower. Really?"

He laughed into my ear. "It's not a pool but it's wet."

"That's true. It *is* wet."

Shawn raised his eyebrows. "Oh, word? Keep it up and see if I don't snatch your little ass up and throw you in the back seat of my car."

"How dare you? I'm a lady."

Shawn laughed. "Is that a no?"

"It's a maybe."

"So how can I turn that maybe into a yes?"

And there it is. Again. The hardest part of this. But I had to make my goal. I had to. I pictured myself in my cap and gown and powered through. "Swimming lessons outside of the pool have a different fee structure."

"I'm listening."

"Double."

"Double?"

"Did I stutter?"

"No, that was pretty clear." He sat back on the couch and stared at me. I held my breath and waited for the no. I could feel it coming. He was about to sprinkle Splenda all over my night.

"You know what? I think I can swing that," he said, and I felt like I'd just won at life.

24

We got back to his place at around midnight. We held hands up the path to the door and I hoped he didn't feel the sweat in my palms. "I never did take you on a tour, did I?" he asked.

"No, but we can do that in the morning."

He smiled at me. "I was thinking the same thing."

We headed straight up the stairs and into his bedroom. It was dark and cave like, exactly what you would expect from a bachelor. Rich mahogany wood, dark hardwood floors, a strangely mesmerizing shade of grey on the walls, and grey bedding with black accents. It didn't look bad at all, just a little masculine for my taste. But it was clean and I have to admit, it was sexy.

Can a place be sexy? I guess when you have everything you could ever want in life, it leaves you relaxed and gives you plenty of free time to think and feel and explore the world with all your senses. Right now, without school or tuition or bills on my mind, I was in another world. A world in which I could thrive. A world in which I could fall in love.

I pushed that thought from my mind and kicked off my shoes. "Is that the bathroom?" I asked as I pointed to the door on my right. "I need to freshen up."

"Yeah, that's it."

I turned to walk toward the bathroom and he called after me, "don't keep me waiting too long."

I peed and did the sniff test and made sure I was on point. I was still a little tipsy but that was good. The liquor was keeping me relaxed. I hadn't had sex in over a year and I definitely wanted to please him. And I wanted to feel good. I deserved to feel good.

I took a few deep breaths and psyched myself up. *You can do this. You're a bad bitch. Go out there and put it on him.* I didn't tell myself to give him his money's worth, but it was in the back of my mind, for sure.

I stepped back out into the bedroom to find it mostly dark, save a few candles Shawn had lit. How romantic.

He was sitting on the edge of the bed staring in my direction. I said nothing as I walked toward him, and his eyes roamed my body like he was starving and I was a whole meal. I reached down and pulled his shirt over his head. Even tipsy and turned on, I still noticed how soft that damn shirt was. It had to be expensive.

He placed his hands in his favorite place, on my

hips, and stared up at me. "You sure?"

I nodded and gently grabbed his face with both hands. We kissed passionately and he moved his hands to unbutton my jeans. He tried to slide them down but you can't do that with tight ass skinny jeans. I kicked myself for not taking them off in the bathroom but it was too late now. I stepped back and eased my jeans down over my hips. He watched me intently.

By the time I was down to just my panties, he was practically salivating. I moved around him and lay down at the head of the bed. He stood, finished undressing, and walked around to the other side. I caught a glimpse of his dick and tried not to panic. Would that thing even fit?

He opened the drawer in his nightstand and pulled out a condom. I watched him unwrap it, pinch the top, and slowly, slowly, slowly roll it down. Like he was teasing me. I could barely stand it anymore.

He laid next to me and rolled to face me. "You good?" he said.

I nodded and he reached down and slid my panties down. I grabbed him and pulled him closer and he rolled on top of me. Just the pressure of his body on mine, the weight of him pressing onto me, felt soooo good. That's the kind of thing you miss when you don't have sex in a while. The weight of human connection.

I gripped his muscular back and kissed his neck. He tried to work his way in and I squeezed my eyes shut and tried to block out the pain. He finally entered me fully and stopped, resting his forehead against mine.

"Are *you* good?" I asked.

"Yeah," he said. "It's just...it's tight down there. I'm not complaining though, trust me."

I giggled and caressed his back with my fingernails. He sighed and began to move, and I moved my hips in unison. I couldn't believe how good it felt. I moaned in his ear and he moaned in mine, and we kissed deeply like we were each other's last meal.

First-time sex can be tricky and awkward but this was neither. I bit his shoulder as he stroked me and he placed a hand at my throat and squeezed lightly, sending me to a place I'd never been.

Then he stopped abruptly.

"What's wrong?" I said breathlessly.

"I'mma make you come tonight."

"It's okay. It might take awhile."

"I don't care."

"I'm fine. It feels good, Shawn."

"I know that. Listen, I need you to focus. It ain't just gon sneak up on you like it does for me. Think about whatever turns you on the most--"

"You."

He grinned and kissed me. "Whatever it is, it's the only thing that should be in your head. Can you do that for me?"

I nodded and he started again, slowly and gently. He kissed me and bit my lip and caressed my tongue with his and I could feel the pressure building. I thought about him, about his face, about his money, about his body, and he stroked me slowly and rhythmically and with an incredible amount of patience. I lost track of time but he had been going for awhile when he ducked his head down to lick my nipple. He sucked gently and finally, the pressure gave way and I came. *Hard.*

I was so overwhelmed I started crying. Happy tears. I hugged him tight as aftershocks pulsed through my body. He kissed me gently on my lips as I came down and when he saw my tears, he brushed them away with his fingers.

"Don't stop," I said.

"I'm just giving you a minute."

My arms and legs felt like jelly. Shawn saw my arm trembling and smiled. "Get it together, Mani. You got at least one more round. You bout to turn that ass over for me."

Well damn. But I sure did turn my ass over with the quickness. He didn't even warn me, he just slammed right into me. I cried out and he seemed to become another person. One I liked.

"Throw that shit back, baby," he growled in my ear, and I obeyed.

"Just like that," he said as he thrust into me. "You sexy as fuck, you know that?"

I whined my answer. I couldn't have spoken actual words even if I wanted to.

"That pussy so wet. You hear that?" he asked. And I did. And it turned me on even more. And then he had the nerve to grab my hair. He pulled it lightly and I was impressed by his restraint. If I could have, I would have grabbed his nearest body part and scratched it until it bled. That's how good it felt.

Instead, I spoke my pleasure and the louder I moaned, the harder he thrust. I was on the verge of screaming when he licked my ear and said, "why were you crying? The dick that good?"

"Yes!" I cried, and he chuckled in my ear.

"Yes what? Don't be shy."

"It's good."

"Don't fucking play with me. What's good?"

The aggression drove me to a level of sexual insanity I had never felt before. I would have done anything for him at that moment. I would have said anything or gone anywhere. "The dick, it's too good. I can't take it."

"You will." He slammed into me, harder and faster, and the sound of our bodies meeting filled the room. "Take this dick."

I didn't want it to end but I could tell by his movements that he was losing control. He was close. And I wanted to talk shit too.

"Fuck me, Shawn."

He groaned and gripped my hips so hard I felt bruised. "Harder. Fuck me, just like that," I whined.

He obliged and not 30 seconds later, he was growling in my ear again as he came. I didn't even want him to pull out. A line had been crossed and walls had come down. I've never taken sex lightly. It's the literal joining of bodies, minds, and souls. Shawn was in me now and I was in him. That meant something to me.

We lay there for awhile breathing in sync with each other and I tried to ignore the little voice in my head that told me not to trust it.

<u>25</u>

Imani

I knew this was gonna happen. I knew I would get caught up. Shawn got in my head and now I was all dizzy and disoriented.

I wanna say it was the sex, because then I would be just one in a sea of women who were struck dumb by some good peen. But it's not just that. I like him. As a person. And he treats me like a queen. And he's *rich*. That's as much an aphrodisiac as any penis.

Day 34 began with me bathing myself in the gigantic black marble shower with three separate shower heads that practically gave me a full body massage.

I stepped out of the shower and onto a grey tile floor to find that Shawn had turned it on. The floor was warm beneath my feet. I wrapped myself in the softest, plushest white robe this side of a 5-star hotel and stepped into a brand new pair of Ugg slippers.

They hugged my feet as I descended the stair-case and padded my way into the kitchen where Chef

Alex was working the stove.

"Good morning," he called to me. "Can I get you anything?"

"Can I have pancakes, please?"

"You can have whatever you like, Miss. Fruit?"

"Yes, whatever you have is fine." I looked around and didn't see Shawn anywhere. "Have you seen Sh--Mr. Jeter?"

Chef Alex chuckled. "I call him Shawn. He's out on the deck."

I flashed him a smile and made my way to the deck. It was just off the living room and the view was gorgeous. I could see the bed where we had our first encounter and the memory made me flush hot.

Shawn was sitting in a deck chair with a Starbucks cup in his hand. "Good morning, Beautiful."

I leaned over and kissed him softly on the lips. "Good morning."

"You good?"

"Good and spoiled. Are you kidding me with that shower? And the heated floor? And this robe?"

Shawn chuckled. "You *should* be spoiled. You deserve it."

Did I? Why? I wondered. What made me so special? "Thank you. So what are you up to today?"

"What are *we* up to?"

I couldn't hide my smile. "Are you saying you wanna spend the day with me?"

He put a hand on my ass and looked up at me. "I would spend every day with you if I could."

My heart skipped a beat. This wasn't good. I was

feeling...feelings. *Only 34 more days,* I reminded my-self. "All day long. That's gonna cost you," I said, trying to sound playful.

Shawn sighed and moved his hand from my ass. "Why don't we just say for the record that I already know that and I'm good for it. Okay?"

"Okay," I said softly, knowing I had irritated him. I needed to get better at that. I leaned down and wrapped my arms around his neck. He leaned his head to the side until it touched the side of my face and we held that position for a moment before he pulled me around and into his lap.

"So what are we doing today? Anything you want."

"Anything?" I said.

"Anything."

I giggled. "Let's watch *Titanic.*"

And that's how we ended up in the theater. Chef Alex brought us homemade pizzas and truffle fries (those were my request) and Shawn mixed us hella drinks at the theater bar. I was on my third Cosmo when my phone vibrated in the pocket of my robe, which I still hadn't changed out of. The words were blurry until I was finally able to focus my eyes.

Where r u? been waiting almost an hr!!!

Shit. I was supposed to meet Farrah for lunch.

Sry. Stuck at shawn's. C u later?

I didn't wait for an answer. I promptly silenced my phone and turned my attention back to the movie.

Shawn reached across his armrest and grabbed

my foot. "Everything okay?"

"Fine," I said. I poked him in the stomach with my big toe and he retaliated by tickling the bottom of my foot. I giggled and screamed like a toddler until tears streamed down my face.

On the screen, Rose was watching a little girl re-live her horrible, wealthy, upper class life while in the theater, Shawn was watching me. He wiped the tears off my face and pulled me into his lap so that I was straddling him. I felt his erection through his sweatpants and my robe. I wanted to grind on it but--ah hell, I went ahead and started grinding on it. He bit his lip and closed his eyes. I pushed my robe open at the front and put his hands on my breasts. He opened his eyes and caressed my nipples. "Let me take my pants off so you can ride me."

"You have condoms down here?"

"I hope you aren't one of those women who does all that wining and grinding until you actually get on the dick. That shit pisses me off. It's false advertising."

"Condoms?"

"All the way upstairs."

He wanted to ask me. He *really* wanted to ask me. I could tell by the look in his eyes. But there was no way I was letting this man sex me raw. Because I was feeling reckless and it's exactly what I wanted him to do. No more drinking for me today, I decided. I needed to keep my head in the game.

"Later, then," I said.

He sighed loudly. "You're right. I'm glad you're

thinking straight. One of us needs to be."

"You're not?"

"Baby, I'm four scotches deep right now. I don't even remember your last name."

Did he just call me baby?

I pecked him on the lips and moved back to my seat so we could finish the movie.

Shawn leaned over. "You want me to take you home later? Or are you staying here with me?"

I debated. I had already missed lunch with Farrah. We were supposed to talk about her upcoming date. Then again, she's a big girl. I found my way on my own; why did I need to drop everything I was doing to hold her hand?

And then there was Bill. I didn't get a chance to respond to his texts which wasn't a good look. Okay, I had a few chances but I chose not to. I was too into Shawn. That's not a bad thing, right? I reminded myself that I was at work, and therefore wasn't actually doing anything wrong. Farrah had missed plenty of our plans due to work. This was the same thing. Right?

Right.

So I spent the night again.

26

His heartbeat soothed me as I drifted in and out of sleep. I was completely relaxed and totally spent. I felt him take in a breath and pause, and I knew he was going to say something. I would have rather slept.

"Can I ask you a personal question?" he said.

"You can. I might not answer it though."

"What made you get into this?"

That wasn't the post-coital pillow talk I was expecting. "Didn't you tell me you were listening to my conversation?"

"So it's just about money?"

"Pretty much."

"Hmm."

I felt like he was judging me, and that wasn't cool at all. "What made *you* get into this? Before me?"

"Just something to do. I never actually hooked up with anybody. I was just browsing."

"Browsing?" I asked with a laugh. "That's one way to look at it."

He paused and I could hear and feel his heart-beat speed up. This conversation wasn't over. "I have another question. Are you seeing anybody else from there?"

"Does it matter?"

"I don't know." That let me know it did matter.

"We've never discussed exclusivity. If that's something you're interested in, we can talk about it."

"Oh. Right. How much?"

I lifted my head to look into his eyes. "Don't be like that."

"That's what this is all about, though, right?"

"It is for me. You knew that going in. Why are you switching up now?"

"I'm not switching up. I just--what's your end game, here?"

"To get my degree. And the only way that's gonna happen is if I can pay my tuition."

He was quiet. I was quiet. It seemed safe so I lay my head back on his chest and threw a thigh over his. He traced circles on my scalp with his fingertips and I dozed again. His voice woke me. "Okay, how about this: I pay your tuition. For the whole year."

I was glad he wasn't looking at me because I've never had much of a poker face. The idea that this could all be over, that I could pay my tuition and pro-pel myself toward my goal...it felt like Christmas and my birthday at the same damn time. I tried my abso-lute best not to show how happy I was at the prospect of getting everything I wanted. Because honestly, I wanted my knight, too.

"I can agree to those terms. Tuition for the year and I don't see anyone during that time."

He leaned his face toward mine and kissed my forehead. "Good."

I smiled up at him and returned to my spot on his chest. I was close to dozing off again when he dropped the bomb.

"And the sugar baby shit? You dead all that. Your profile gotta come down ASAP."

I sat up and hugged the sheet to my bare breasts, frowning in confusion. "Wait, that's going a little far. I agreed not to see anybody else."

"Right. So why would you need to keep your profile up?"

"Because this right here isn't forever. It's for a year. But after that year is up, I still have to pay my rent."

He sat up and leaned back against the headboard. "After the year is up, you'll have your degree and my connections. And hell, I might invest in your ventures if I see some potential there."

"So nothing concrete, just hopes and wishes."

"Imani--"

"I can't eat hopes and wishes, Shawn."

"No but you can trust me when I say I'll do everything I can to make sure you're straight. You won't have to worry about rent, baby girl. Trust me."

But I didn't trust him. I barely even knew him. "I'm not comfortable with...having to obey you."

"Obey? What are you talking about?"

"I've been in a relationship that was--"

"Imani--"

"He was very controlling--"

"Imani--"

"And I'm very sensitive to--"

"Imani!"

I startled and stopped talking. I hadn't even been looking at him when I was rambling. "Yes?"

"I'm not trying to control you. I guess I'm just trying to navigate...whatever this is," he said, pointing back and forth between us.

"It's an...arrangement."

I could swear he looked at me with sadness in his eyes. "That's it?"

"Well...no. Look, I don't know how to do this either, but I know I don't wanna be in a relationship with rules on who I can talk to and what websites I can post on."

"That's not..." he paused, clearly frustrated. "I don't know where to go from here. It doesn't make sense to keep doing meetings or appointments or whatever the fuck you tell yourself this is to keep from admitting you have feelings for me."

"It doesn't make sense to *you*. It makes perfect sense for *me*."

"So what are you saying?"

"Shawn, I have a goal. I need to make my goal, but it has to be on my terms."

He shook his head and laughed sarcastically. "I'm lost as fuck right now. I have no idea what you want."

"I wanna earn the money to pay my tuition

without having a million strings attached."

"It's just one little string. And that's not the way the world works, baby girl."

"Well enlighten me, then."

"Money ain't free. It always comes with stipulations. You need to learn that now before you get out there in the real world with niggas who aren't as accommodating as me."

I didn't respond. That was a lesson I'd already learned. The hard way.

His face softened and he grabbed my hand. "I wanna help you, Mani. I have the means to help you. But I'm also feeling you. And for whatever reason, those two things don't match in your mind."

"I'm sorry. I just can't do it your way."

He dropped my hand. "And I can't do it yours."

That's the way we left it. Shawn laid back down and I did the same, except I stayed on my side of the bed and played Solitaire on my phone, all traces of sleep gone.

What the hell is wrong with me?

We didn't say much in the morning. The chef made a delicious breakfast but I barely tasted a thing. The ride home was equally uneventful, and by the time the Porsche pulled up to my building, I was near tears.

Shawn put the car in park and we sat there for awhile listening to the radio. I asked myself, over and over, if I was doing the right thing, and each time, I told myself yes. But Shawn looked sad, I felt sick, and I didn't wanna get out of the car.

"Oh, before I forget," he said as he reached in the glove box, "here's your, uh, your payment."

He handed me a standard office envelope. I thought it would be in poor taste to count it so I simply slid it into my purse and muttered, "thank you."

"You're very welcome. I hope it helps you."

I nodded. "These last few days were everything."

"Agree."

"Are we gonna see each other again?" I asked, silently pleading with him to say yes.

"I guess I'll hit you up on the site if I wanna schedule an appointment."

I tilted my head. "Shawn. Don't be like that." No matter how old they are, men always act like little boys when they don't get their way.

"I'm just trying to operate within your parameters. I don't wanna control you."

"Don't be petty."

"Nah, I'm straight. Take care of yourself, alright?"

"So that's it?"

He sighed and stared out the window. "It doesn't have to be."

"I don't think we'll ever see eye to eye on this."

He continued to stare out the window. I grabbed his face gently and turned it toward me. "Are you sure we can't just do what we've been doing?"

He leaned his head away from my grasp. "It's not enough for me."

He still opened my door and hugged me but it

wasn't the same. And when he drove away without a wave or even a look, I knew he was lost to me.

27

Imani is not built for this sugar baby shit. And really, neither am I. And how do I know this? I know this because we're both inclined to do the exact opposite of what you're supposed to do in arrangements like these.

I wanna go ahead and pay her tuition, her student loans, her car, and whatever else is dragging her down. And I've already made inquiries on her behalf with friends of mine in the industry. I even paid for her Global Elite membership. When she's ready, all she has to do is take the course. I know it seems like I'm jumping the gun, but I'm not a thinker, I'm a doer. And when I get around people who want to better themselves, I go from 0 to 60 real quick.

The point is, I don't think that's in the sugar daddy playbook. I think you're supposed to ration out the gifts and payments in the same way she rations out the sex. Like I said, I'm not really interested in all that. All she has to do is ask and it's hers.

She won't ask.

Imani is a sweetheart, but she's also reached the green young age of 23 without having been taught how to depend on other people. She's become one of those dreaded independent women who don't need niggas for shit. She'd rather do this and pretend like it's an honest day's work than let me be her man and take care of her.

All I asked her to do was take her profile down. That's not too much, right? What man wants to see his lady on a website for what is basically glorified prostitution? And look, I'm not knocking it. Every man on this earth pays for sex. We single men pay in dinners and drinks and money spent here and there on flowers or candy or clothes or whatever that particular woman's favorite trinkets are. And don't even fool yourself: married men pay, too. Their first installment is a diamond and the rest of their payments are spread out over the rest of their lives.

I pulled into my garage and turned the car off. I'd just dropped her off. She didn't even look back after she got out of the car, and that pissed me off. Had she been faking? I thought she was feeling me too. I know the sex was on point. What, exactly, did I do so wrong that she was willing to cut things off completely?

I trudged into the house and tossed my keys on the table. See, this is the kinda shit that makes a man act out. It's a good thing I'm too old for strip club and getting high with the boys type tantrums. At my age, you just learn the lesson and move the fuck on.

Maybe it was my fault. She was always honest

about who she was. And instead of listening to her the first time, I thought it was something it wasn't. I opened my heart to her.

Oh well. Won't make that mistake again.

28

I knocked softly in case she was asleep. "Farrah? Farrah?"

There was no telltale snoring so I knew she was awake. I got home at around noon and I could swear she ran to her room when she heard my key in the lock. The smell of her lotion lingered in the living room, along with the smell of Doritos.

She was still mad. I had no doubt about that. But I wasn't sure if I should give her space or badger her into talking to me. Farrah is sensitive; she may see me giving her space and assume I don't care about her feelings. Gotta tread lightly with her.

I stood at the door for almost five minutes but she never came.

Oh well. I made my way into my bedroom and plopped down on my bed. I didn't have the energy for heartfelt apologies, anyway. I was dealing with my own shit.

My eyes welled up with tears as I thought about Shawn. My knight. What possessed me to sabotage our growing relationship? The last two days with him had been some of the best I've ever had with a man, and I promptly screwed it all up. And for what?

Oh, right. My goal.

Was it bullshit? I don't know. I thought I was doing the right thing, I really did. But now I wasn't so sure.

I had him. He was ready to pay my whole tuition bill and all he wanted in return was loyalty. But I couldn't do it. Maybe I'm too damaged. Maybe I'm afraid.

Tears crawled their way to my ears as I lay on my bed. It was day 31 and I had a little cash on hand but I was still so far away.

I sat up and wiped my face. Crying wouldn't get me closer to my goal. Only one thing would. Getting back to work.

I plugged my phone into the charger and scrolled through my text messages. I was afraid to read Bill's but when I pulled them up, I was relieved.

Hey, beautiful. Just wanted to touch bases.

The second one was a little iffy but still not so bad I couldn't salvage it.

***I guess you're busy. Just say hello
when you have the time.***

Cool. I could do that. I was typing when Farrah knocked on the door.

"Come in."

She entered with a scowl on her face. "What happened to you?"

I finished texting Bill. "I don't wanna talk about

it."

"Nuh uh. You gotta do better than that. You stood me up, heffa."

"I know, I'm sorry. I was with Shawn."

She sat across from me on the bed. "I know that. You still could have called or texted though."

"I know. I was trifling. And you know I hate trifling."

"Me too. So did everything go okay?"

I shook my head and filled her in on my epic screw-up.

"Titanic?" she asked with a grin.

"That's all you got from this?"

"It's so cute though."

"Whatever."

"Sorry, but it sounds like y'all were vibing a little bit."

"More than a little bit. And girl, the sex."

She leaned toward me and took a deep breath.

"Bananas. I can't even--just trust me. He may be old but he was ready."

She clapped her hands together. "Biiiiitch. I'm so glad you took my advice."

"Did I mess things up?"

"If it was me, I'd say yes. But it's you, and you have your own issues. I understand why you reacted the way you did."

"Really?"

"Yeah. You have to do what feels right to you. Does it feel right?"

Good question. "I don't know. I keep going back

and forth."

Farrah sighed. "Well, I support you in whatever you decide. Now, can we talk about me?"

I chuckled. "Go."

"Okay, so Jacob wants to take me to Tilt."

"Tilt? Isn't that a sex club?"

"No, no, it's a regular club but it has...booths."

"I don't know, Farrah. That's a lot for a first date."

"You think so?"

"Did you ever go online and do your research?"

"We were supposed to do that over lunch but you stood me up, remember?"

"Oh. Right. Sorry. Just--"

My phone buzzed at that moment. I ignored it. Farrah deserved my undivided attention now. "When is the date again?"

"Two days. I told you this already!"

But I wasn't listening. Again. Because my phone buzzed again. The first buzz was Shawn. The second was Bill.

I ignored Shawn's and went straight to Bill's, which was about setting up a date for Friday, the same day as Farrah's date. I responded with an enthusiastic yes and felt a small bit of relief. Maybe things were salvageable after all.

I looked up and Farrah was gone.

I met Bill at Urbanity. I had on a simple black dress. Nothing fancy, but it was new and much better quality than anything else in my closet. On my feet,

I wore my Louboutins. I felt kind of grimy wearing them on a date with another man; I suppose I'll always think of them as Shawn's shoes. But truly, they were mine. That's how gifts work. So I got over myself.

He was at the bar watching the door when I made my entrance. As soon as I hit the hostess station, he stood to greet me.

"You clean up good," he said as he kissed my cheek.

"Thank you. It's been so long since I saw you. It feels like it, at least."

"Doesn't it? Next time don't keep me waiting so long," he said with a sly smile. He looked nice and distinguished in a grey suit. No tie, but he didn't need one.

I wasn't sure how to respond to that little mini-scolding so I waited a few beats and let it pass. "What's good here?" I asked.

"You, from where I'm sitting."

Okay then, Bill. I giggled and covered my mouth. "What got into you today?"

He laughed and relaxed. "Look, I'm three beers in. It's been a long week."

"Well you can tell me all about it over dinner."

The hostess led us to our seats and I enjoyed the stares we got as we moved past each table. Once we were seated, I leaned closer and with a smile, I whispered, "tell me all about it."

Bill droned on and on about a contractor who's doing work on his house and some woman at work who made a bad call that cost his company $40,000. I was half listening because the peach martini was hitting and I honestly didn't care that much. But I made sure I smiled and laughed and nodded along periodically. I'm a good listener but I'm even better at pretending I'm listening.

I fake smiled at his stories but I was somewhere else. I hadn't talked to my parents since that spaghetti dinner. Part of it was guilt over getting them in that predicament and the other part was guilt over my secret lifestyle. I mean, I had a whole other life they knew nothing about, and it wasn't one I was proud of.

And then there was Shawn. Trust issues are a mean bitch. Shawn wasn't Eric. My head knew that but my heart and my spirit weren't so wise. And the little voice in my head that kept telling me not to trust him--she wasn't helping matters, either.

I fake laughed when Bill laughed. I don't even know what the fuck he'd said. And then the fake smile froze on my face as I saw someone I knew walk in the door. Two someones.

It was my knight. And on his arm? The fucking Blasian Amazon.

<u>29</u>

Shawn

I remember the first time Pop met Joya. He didn't seem all that impressed by her looks which, if I'm being honest, shit on 75% of the women I've ever gone out with. He told me later on that night that he thought she was a good catch. "Wife material," he'd said. I asked him how he knew that and--I'll never forget this--he said, "she's malleable."

I knew what malleable meant but I remember being dumbstruck. "What do you mean?" I'd asked him, genuinely confused and on the verge of being offended on her behalf.

"Just keep living," he'd said with a wink.

I did keep living, and now that I'm a grown ass man with experience, I know exactly what he meant. But a small part of me wondered if that's what he saw in my mother. Because that would make me respect him less. But I've never asked. I guess I don't wanna know.

But here I was on a Friday night, sitting in the car next to Joya the Malleable, on the way to dinner.

The small talk came easy and she still looked just as good as she did the day we met. I can't speak for her Filipino grandfather's side but her black mama's side was in no danger of cracking.

"Is this new?" she asked, gesturing to the inside of the car.

"Nah, I've had this a few years."

"I'm surprised. You used to change cars like you changed underwear."

"I was young and dumb, that's all."

She sucked her teeth. "You're still young. And so am I. At least that's what I tell myself when I look in the mirror."

She was trying to sound playful but I knew there was some feeling behind those words. A 36-year-old black woman with a great career, plenty of money, and a good head on her shoulders is still not complete without a family, let society tell it.

"You still got it, Joya. Trust."

She smiled her thanks and I hoped that made her feel better. I can't have an insecure woman on my arm. It's an automatic downgrade for me.

We pulled up and valeted, and she grabbed my hand as we entered the restaurant. I didn't mind; she had on stilettos.

We hit the hostess station and I asked for Fernando, the owner, because I hadn't made reservations. I grabbed a matchbook and a toothpick as we waited and offered to get Joya a drink from the bar. She declined.

I scanned the room to see if there was anyone

there I knew. I was almost done scanning when I saw her.

Imani.

She was sitting at a table with some white nigga, laughing and giggling and shit like they were together. *My* Imani.

Who the fuck was this dude? Another sugar daddy? Is that why she didn't wanna take her profile down, because she was already seeing other men like she was seeing me? The thought of her and that white dude having sex made my stomach turn.

"It's taking longer than I thought. Did you wanna go somewhere else?" I asked Joya, damn near panicked. But before she could answer, a heavy hand slapped me on the back.

"Shawn!" said Fernando as I turned around.

"Nando, what's good, man?"

"It's about time you came by!"

"Man, I stay busy. You know how it is."

"I hear you. And who is this lovely woman?" he asked.

"This is Joya. We're old friends from college."

"I should have gone to college," Fernando said before kissing Joya's hand. She giggled and said, "pleasure to meet you."

"Let's get you two a table," he said, his eyes not leaving Joya's face. I figured it was too late to back out now so I grabbed Joya's hand and moved her in front of me. I kept my right hand on her back as he walked. A part of me hoped we passed Imani's table and luckily, we passed right by it.

It was worth it to see the look on her face. I'm not a petty person by nature but I was still reeling from her rejection of me. What can I say? I'm only human.

As soon as she saw us, her face fell. Joya passed right by her, which made it even better because that meant she didn't even remember meeting her. I wanted Imani to feel insignificant. I wanted her to feel small. I passed her too, without even looking at her.

We ended up by the picture window and I had two great views. One of the city, and the other of Imani's table. Her back was to me so I could look at them all night without her knowing. Perfect.

Dinner was uneventful. I had the lamb sliders and Joya had a piece of salmon that looked more leathery than the purse she was carrying. Every time I snuck a glance at Imani's table, the white dude was laughing or smiling in her face. Fake ass white boy. Imani ain't that damn funny.

"Give me another one of these," I said to our waitress as I shook my empty scotch glass at her.

"You alright?" Joya asked. She looked worried.

"I'm fine. I'm *good*."

She didn't seem convinced. "Did you wanna do something after this? Maybe go see some jazz or something?"

I had forgotten she loves jazz. But truth be told, I wasn't interested in prolonging our date. Not with Imani and Donald Trump over there giggling and shit.

The waitress brought my scotch and I downed

it in three gulps. Joya sat back and stared at me. "We don't have to do that. We can do something else if you want. I'm open to whatever."

Joya the Malleable.

Imani and ol' boy left about ten minutes later and he had the nerve to have his hand on the small of her back. Hold up--and she was wearing my shoes! The Louboutins I bought her! What kind of shit is that? The fuck. An image popped in my head just then. Those shoes wrapped around his waist as he--

"Did you hear me?" Joya was saying. "Do you want dessert?"

I shook my head, as much to answer her as to clear that hideous image from my mind. "I'm good. Just bring the check," I said to the waitress who was hovering over me.

"Look, Joya, I'm a little distracted tonight. I apologize for being off my game. I'm just going through some things right now."

"Yeah, I figured. You wanna talk about it?"

"I don't think you wanna hear about my woman problems."

"It's fine. I'm your friend. I'm here to listen if you need me to."

See, this is why I can't be with Joya. There's not a damn thing challenging about her. She's a dime but she has no idea how to wield that power. It's a complete turnoff. I looked at her and felt nothing but disgust. How could such a smart woman be so simple?

"Nah, you don't wanna hear it. We're on a date. I can't do that to you." I was practically begging her to woman up.

She reached over and touched my hand. "I'm here for you, Shawn. Whatever you need."

So she was still willing to fuck me after I'd spent the entire night tipsy and checked out. Pathetic. "I just need...I need to go home and sleep this off. I'm too old to be hungover," I said with a chuckle, hoping to take some of the sting out of my rejection.

"Oh. It's cool. I understand." She smiled that million-dollar smile and I felt like shit.

I walked her to her door and had to muster up the decency to give her a goodnight kiss so she wouldn't feel completely rejected. Any other night, at any other time, and I would have been inside that door and them drawls with no hesitation. But it was that damn Imani. She was still in my head.

I sat in my car and waited for Joya to flick the light. And then I stewed. And wondered if Imani went home after her date or if she was still hanging with ol' boy. And then I got angry.

I was still a little tipsy so I'm gonna blame what happened next on the alcohol.

<u>*30*</u>

I cannot *believe* Joya the Blasian fucking Amazon showed up with my knight on her arm. The date had been going so well before they showed up and ruined everything.

My stomach dropped when I saw them and I completely lost my appetite. And then he had the nerve to parade her past my table and not even speak!

Bill noticed my distress immediately. "Hey, are you okay? You kinda spaced out there for a minute. Am I boring you with my work story?"

"No! I'm sorry, I just thought I saw somebody I knew but it wasn't her. What were you saying?"

Bill blathered on and I seethed for awhile before I decided I was being stupid. I had cut him loose. I had my chance and I blew it, and now he was free to date whoever he wanted.

It sounded good in my head but my heart was another story. Why did it have to be *her*? That day on the boat, he told me all about how his father had been trying to get Joya and him together for years. She was wife material, according to Mr. Jeter. Her with her perfect teeth and law degree and prestigious job at a prestigious law firm. And what was I? Just a five-year student at a state school who takes money from rich men just to pay my tuition. If I had a son, I'd want him to marry a Joya, too.

I zoned back in on Bill and heard him talking about his daughter's horse. "Bill, I'm sorry. I don't mean to interrupt you but we need to discuss something."

"Okay," he said, his forehead creased with concern.

"I'm really enjoying our time together and everything but we need to discuss our arrangement. Or lack thereof."

Bill was quiet for a moment before nodding. "Make me an offer."

"I'd like to do a pay-per-meet. $500 for regular outings. Other...things will be open for negotiation."

"Five-hundred is pretty steep."

Shit. I'd pushed too far. I started to speak but remembered something the girls said. There were suckers, Splendas, and negotiators. Bill was a negotiator.

He stared and waited for me to crack but I didn't. He finally spoke again. "I can do three-fifty."

"Four hundred."

Bill smiled at me and raised his glass. "Four hundred."

I raised mine and took a long swig. I had managed to forget Shawn and the Amazon for a moment because I had just gotten what I wanted. But the victory was short-lived because I knew he was back there somewhere with her, laughing and flirting and staring at her titties like he used to do with me.

We left and Bill walked me to my car. I debated going back to his place and speeding things up. But in the end, I knew I would be too distracted to be good company and frankly, I wasn't ready anyway. I did kiss him goodnight though and it was...nice. His lips were thin but they were soft. I was impressed. The stack of cash in my hand was the cherry on top.

The pleasure was short-lived. By the time I got home, I was good and pissed. At Shawn, at the Amazon, but mostly at myself.

I was only inside for a minute when I heard a soft knock at the door.

31

Shawn

The second she opened the door, I lost all traces of pisstivity. The only thing I wanted was her.

She didn't seem all that surprised to see me and I was glad. I wasn't trying to scare her. I only wanted to talk.

"What the hell are you doing here?" she asked.

"Can I come in?"

"Not until you tell me why you're here." She frowned. "Don't you have a date to get back to?"

Oh shit, I had her. I tried not to smile as I realized she was pissed about Joya. And if she was pissed, that meant she was still invested. "My date is over. Where's Chad?"

"Chad?"

"Brad? Brett? I don't know that nigga's name."

Her face relaxed and she laughed. At me. "Oh, so that's why you came. You're jealous."

"That's not why."

"Then why?"

"Let me in, Mani. It's hot out here."

She crossed her arms and stared at me for a minute and I felt like an idiot. But she finally stepped aside and allowed me through the door and I felt like I won. All the fight went out of me and I just wanted her.

I stood in the tiny living room and waited for her to make a move. She gestured toward the couch. "You want something to drink?"

I sat and patted the cushion next to me. "Nah, I'm good. Sit down and let me talk to you for a second."

She obliged and I took a deep breath and realized I didn't know exactly what to say to this woman.

I looked around. "This is nice."

She rolled her eyes and crossed those arms again. "What do you want, Shawn? I know you didn't come here to evaluate my decor."

"So it's like that?"

"Apparently it is. You out here on dates with the woman your father wants you to marry and ignoring me when you see me. What the hell was that?"

"I thought I was being polite and shit. I didn't wanna interrupt your date with Joe Biden."

She stared at me coldly. "You're way too old to be this petty."

That was the first time she'd ever insulted my age and it triggered something I didn't realize was there. Now I was pissed again. "You know what? Fuck you."

She jumped to her feet. "Fuck you, too! And get the fuck out my house."

I stood slowly so that I didn't alarm her. She stared at me with a defiant look in her eyes and it was all I could stand. I grabbed her by the waist and yanked her toward me. She hesitated for a moment before smashing her face into mine, letting me know she was on the exact same page.

My tongue roamed her mouth and she grabbed the back of my head and moaned into my mouth. Something came over me and I pushed her away. "Take that dress off and throw that shit away."

She stared at me in disbelief. "I just got this."

"I don't give a fuck. I'll buy you another one."

She blinked a few times and she looked like she wanted to argue but then she lifted that tainted dress over her head and did exactly as I said.

I took my shirt off as she walked back toward me and I was both excited and disturbed to see she wasn't wearing any panties.

She grabbed the throw blanket off the couch and threw it on the floor as I got the last of my clothes off. Neither of us hesitated for a second, we just got right to it, condoms be damned.

I slid right in and she immediately used her body weight to roll me over. She leaned down and kissed me again, and then she rode me like a thoroughbred. I was pleasantly surprised to learn she was most definitely not one of those false advertising chicks. She knew what the fuck she was doing.

I grabbed her hips as they rolled and watched the sweat glistening on her body. Her eyes rolled back and breasts bounced in my face. I managed to catch one in my mouth and as I caressed her nipple with my tongue, I felt her walls clinch around me and I knew she was close. I gently nipped her breast with my teeth and she yelled out as she came. She fell on top of me and as her pussy throbbed around me, she purred in my ear and it was the sweetest sound I'd ever heard. I grabbed a fistful of hair and pulled her head up so I could see her face as I thrust myself deeper.

"Shawwwwwwwn," she whined.

"What, baby?"

"What is that? You're...you're hitting something."

"That's your spot."

She moaned something unintelligible and I stroked harder.

"Yesssss, right there. That feels so good," she whined, and I slowed down a little. She might have been on top but I was the one in control.

I let go of her hair and gripped her ass. I moved her the way I wanted her and she let herself be moved. Once I was sure she was good, I let go and my own orgasm shot deep inside of her. She collapsed on top of me again and that's where we stayed.

We lay there panting and sweaty. I don't know what she was thinking but she seemed content. I kissed her forehead and she put her hand on my face, caressing it softly while she stared deep into my eyes. I swear I felt completely lost in her, but in the best way.

I didn't know how to verbalize what I was feeling, and I wasn't even sure I wanted to. Yet. I just savored the moment.

"Shit," she said. "My roommate."

That made me laugh. "If she's here, she just got to know us real well as a couple."

Imani giggled. "I don't think she's here. She might be on a date, actually."

"Maybe we should go in your room just in case she brings homeboy back here."

She pouted. "I don't feel like moving."

"Me either. I could stay here forever."

Shit. Why did I say that? Next I'll be in the ocean hanging from the side of a raft freezing my ass off.

I took a deep breath. "I'm sorry for what I said earlier. I don't usually talk to women that way. My mama taught me better than that."

"You're gonna have to make it up to me."

"What you want me to do?"

She smiled and stood to her feet, the throw blanket wrapped around her body. She grabbed my hand and pulled me down the short hallway and into a small bedroom. She closed the door and dropped the blanket. "I want you to apologize to me properly."

Gladly.

She laid me down on her bed and crawled up until she was sitting on my face. I'm nasty and I've always been nasty so I was down for whatever. Put it in front of me and I'll bury my whole face in it. I gripped her hips and held her down while I ate her out and it was so good to her, she actually banged her hands on the wall. I hoped her neighbors were cool.

When I was coming up, eating pussy was

frowned upon. I never understood that. How could you not want to make a woman scream? What man doesn't love the feeling of her fingernails digging into your scalp and her thighs squeezing your face? Who doesn't like catching them when they run from it? And when she comes? Nothing like it in this world.

Afterward, we both fell asleep, side by side on her small but comfortable bed. I woke first but she spoke first.

"I don't know how to do this."

"Do what?"

"A relationship with such...lopsided power dynamics. It scares me. Because of my past."

"Whoever he was, I ain't him."

"I know that, but the...specter of him still haunts me."

"I understand that. I'm *trying* to understand that. But how will you ever be happy if you can't move on?"

"You don't know what I went through."

I hate baggage. Everybody has it, I know this, but women's baggage is so much fucking heavier. "So what do you need from me? Help me understand."

"I need you to ease up on the regulations."

"That's a real strong word for a simple request. I'll gladly take my profile down."

"That's different."

"How is that different?"

She signed. "Like I told you before. I have a goal and I need to do all of this on my own terms. I have to. It's the one thing I know for sure."

I rubbed my eyes and tried not to show how frustrated I was. "So I guess we're right back where we left off, then."

"I guess so."

I dressed in silence. She watched me from the bed, probably hoping I'd change my mind. But there wouldn't be any negotiation about this.

She may have seen this as a dick move, or maybe one last petty power play on my part, but a deal's a deal. Just before I walked out the door, I took $500 cash from my wallet and left it on her desk.

32

Imani

I was laying in my bed stewing over the conversation I'd just had with Shawn when my phone rang. I hoped it was Farrah, but it wasn't. It was Fran.

"Hey Fran, what's up?"

"Arianna's in labor."

I sat up and put my feet flat on the floor to ground myself. I had been floating in confusion ever since Shawn walked out my door. "OMG, for real? Right now?"

"Yes, now."

"Do I have time to get there before she has it?"

"She's at seven centimeters now, but the last few go quick."

"Okay, which hospital?"

"Eastside Regional."

"I'm leaving now," I said breathlessly. I dressed in record time and grabbed a banana on my way out the door. Farrah's door was still closed so I assumed she came home at some point and went to bed. I would call her from the hospital.

We could hear Arianna screaming all the way in the waiting room.

"Is she doing this without drugs?" I asked, my eyes wide with fear.

Ms. James, Fran's mother, chuckled. "If she is, it serves her right."

"That's so mean," I said with a giggle. Ms. James is quite a character. She has bright red hair, and not the natural red Fran has. She dyes her hair Bozo red. She also swears White Diamonds like it's going out of style. Although I guess it actually *is* out of style.

Finally, at long last, the baby stopped torturing poor Arianna and dove into the world headfirst, loud and mad. I stood at the door to her hospital room and teared up. Arianna was like a baby sister to me, or maybe a niece. Whatever I called her, I loved her like she was family. And now our family had a new member.

Fran poked her head out. "It's a boy and he's nice and healthy. Eight pounds, eleven ounces, and big lungs, as you can hear."

I clapped my hands together and grabbed the little bear I had bought at CVS on the way there. "Give this to her for me," I said, but Fran shook her head.

"You can give it to her yourself. They said give them ten minutes to get them all cleaned up."

Ten minutes felt like forever, but the door finally opened and Fran beckoned for us to come.

I hung back and let blood family go first and then I made my way into the room. On very rare occasions when I'm around Fran's people, I'm acutely aware of being the only black face in a sea of white folks. This was one such time, but it didn't bother me. I just wanted to see that baby.

He was pink and plump and looked like an alien, but all babies need time to cook before they're cute. I congratulated Arianna, who looked completely shell-shocked and bewildered. She remembered her courtesies well enough to say she loved the bear and was happy to see me but I could tell she was in a daze.

I hung around for a little while until Arianna decided to try breastfeeding. Nobody wanted to see that so we all made our way to the waiting room. Even Fran, who said she needed some air.

She and I sat together at a table. "Do you want some coffee or something to eat? I can run to the gift shop or one of the restaurants around here," I told her.

"You're so sweet. But don't worry about it. John's gonna do Door Dash in a little while."

"So how are you feeling, Grandma?" I asked with a grin.

"I never thought I would embrace that title. I thought I'd insist on being called Nana. But you know what? I think I like it."

"Well I was joking. You definitely don't look like a grandma."

"Oh, shut up. I'm a GILF and you know it."

We laughed at that and Fran sat back and let out a long sigh. "She was a champ. I had drugs both times and loved it."

"Yeah, that's my plan. I have nothing to prove to anybody."

"Exactly. But I'm proud of her."

"Does he have a name?"

Fran sighed again. "Not yet. Well, she has a first name. Andrew. But she's still debating the last name. She's not even sure she wants his name on the birth certificate."

"Oh, yeah. Was he here at any point?"

"Nope. Just his daddy and his mama. They're nice people. I don't know how they raised such a loser." She looked down at her feet. "I guess I'm one to talk."

I grabbed her hand. "Don't do that. Arianna is a nice girl and you did a good job with her. Teenagers have sex, and it has nothing to do with what their parents do or don't do. Alright?"

"That's what people say."

"And people are right. I had sex at sixteen. I'm sure you did too. Most of us started in our teens. It doesn't make us bad kids."

Fran nodded. "I needed to hear that."

We sat together for awhile and watched the hustle and bustle of the hospital happen around us.

"Hey," Fran said, "what's been going on with you?"

"How much time you got?"

I filled her in on all, and I do mean all of the details. By the time I was done, she was shaking her head. "I don't know whether to pat you on the back or punch you in the face."

"What? Why?"

"Are you kidding? You got your whale. Your big fish. That's what Shawn is. That's what the girls hope this whole thing results in. Most of them work for years before they hook their big fish. You had it, and you turned it down."

"So I screwed up?"

"Yeeeeeeesssss!" she said, her voice carrying throughout the waiting room. I looked around in embarrassment but nobody was paying Fran any mind.

"I was expecting a pat on the back, if I'm being honest."

"That's because you're just as brand new as my little grandbaby. When you hook your fish, you put your pole away."

That sunk in a little. "But that's giving him too much control. Isn't it?"

"According to who? Listen, this is the game. If you aren't cut out for it, best quit now while you still have your innocence. Find you a nice middle class working man and make a cute little family. Otherwise, you need to develop the stomach for the reality of this lifestyle. And you don't have that yet. If you only knew..."

"I'm listening. Tell me."

"I don't have time to get into it right now. But trust me when I say this: you and Shawn? That's a best case scenario. You better jump on that, and fast."

Fran excused herself to attend to Arianna and I sat there and pondered her wise words. Then my phone rang. I didn't recognize the number but I answered anyway.

"Hello?"

"Farrah's in the hospital." I recognized the voice as belonging to Farrah's sister Felicia.

"Oh my God, what happened?"

"She was on a blind date or something and the guy put his hands on her!"

My heart sank as I realized this was what Fran had been hinting at. This was the reality of the lifestyle.

$$33$$

It was quite a coincidence that Farrah was also at Eastside Regional. Her room was in a different wing though, about a five-minute walk from labor and delivery.

I didn't walk. I ran straight there in a panic, my heart racing, my mouth dry. All I could think about was how I had failed her.

Felicia stood when she saw me. "That was quick," she said.

I paused to catch my breath. "A friend of mine had her baby today."

"Well, Farrah's okay. You can go in if you want. I'm waiting for my mom to get here."

I nodded and inched my way toward room 205. The guilt was eating me alive and the fear wasn't too far behind. Would she be all battered and bruised? Or worse? What had that man done to my best friend?

I opened the door and Farrah turned her head toward me. She had been staring out the window. I said a silent prayer of thanks that she didn't look too bad. Her right eye was purple and there were dark blue splotches on her right cheek. Other than that, she seemed okay.

"Farrah...I'm so sorry," I said as I broke down in tears.

She was calm. "I should have listened to you, Mani."

"Shhh, don't say that. You didn't do anything wrong."

"Yes I did. I got greedy and didn't listen to my gut. Or you."

"So...what happened."

She took a deep breath. "The guy, Jacob, the one I told you about. He was trying to get me to have sex with him. I told him no and he got mad. We were in his car--"

"You rode in his car?"

"I know." She shook her head and tears filled her big brown eyes. "He punched me and choked me until I passed out. See, look," she said, lifting her head and pointing to her neck. I gasped in shock at the bright red and purple splotches on her neck. I could actually see his fingerprints.

"There was no way you could have known he was a psycho, Farrah. It's not your fault."

She shook her head and a tear slid down the side of her face.

This was bad. I didn't wanna ask it but I had to. "Why were you so set on doing this? Your family has money."

She shook her head and looked at the ceiling. "I don't know. I guess I just wanted to feel powerful." She grabbed a tissue from the box on the side table. "Like you."

That did not compute. "Me?"

"Yeah. Your life might not be perfect but you're so strong and determined. And you fix shit. You know? My life doesn't challenge me. It doesn't make me better. I don't have lessons to learn. It's boring and there aren't any wins. I'll gladly deal with a few losses if it means I get to feel like I won sometimes."

I was speechless. "Farrah--"

"You don't get it, I know."

"I love you but you sound crazy. Do you know how many times I've envied you and how easy your life is? I would give anything to not have to worry about tuition or gas or getting my phone turned off. There's nothing fun about any of that. There's nothing fun about the struggle."

She shook her head. "Forget it. You just don't understand."

It was true. I didn't. And I felt bad about that. So I changed the subject. "Did they catch him?"

"I don't know. The police haven't even taken my statement yet. I woke up here and haven't heard any-thing."

That wouldn't do. "What's his full name?"

"Jacob Andretti. That's what he told me. Who knows if that's even right."

"I thought you found him on LinkedIn."

Farrah looked down and shook her head.

"Alright. It's okay. Look, I'm here now. What do you need from me?"

"Look at us. Switching roles," she said with a sad smile.

"Do you need anything? Are you hungry? Thirsty? What can I do?"

"I'll be fine. Just sit with me until my mom gets here."

I threw my purse on the table and pulled my chair over to the bed. We sat and talked like it was a normal day, but inside I was boiling with anger. No, rage. Mr. Andretti had triggered something in me that I hadn't felt in a long time. I wasn't gonna stop until he paid for this. Bet that.

<u>*34*</u>

Imani

Bill took me golfing on day 26, two days after Farrah's attack. I know it seems like that was too soon but she was fine. Physically, at least. And I was on a mission that, if successful, would see that Mr. Andretti got dealt with.

Bill made the rounds at the club and introduced me to several older white folks. He called me his lady friend and they all seemed genuinely pleased to meet me. They asked me if I'd ever been there, if I played, if I was going to take lessons, and if I was enjoying myself. I played along and said what I was supposed to say but my heart wasn't in any of this. And I didn't give a single shit about golf. Bill didn't know that, though. I pretended to listen and learn and even hit a few but I was steady plotting. Steady planning. Waiting for the right time.

That time finally came over cocktails in the lounge. It was a nice place, although I didn't really have anything to compare it to as golf course lounges go. The drinks were good and strong though.

"So do you guys really make deals out there like we poor people think?"

Bill laughed. He seemed to enjoy my peasant jokes. "It happens. But mostly it's a lot of networking and vetting. That's something you'll need to learn how to do once you get into real estate."

"What are you looking for when you're vetting people?" I asked innocently.

"Can he handle himself on the golf course, did he go to the right school, who's he married to, who are his people. Things like that. Intangible, informal signs that this person is worth doing business with."

"Interesting."

"I suppose you could abridge what I just said with one word: snobbery," he said with a laugh. "That's all it is, but we take it very seriously."

"I get it." I took a sip of my bourbon and pretended to think. "Have you ever had an imposter get in? Like a Don Draper type?"

Bill was amused. "Would never happen."

"Yeah but how would you know? Do you background check these people?"

"No need. It only takes 60 seconds of talking for you to know a person's background, particularly if they're trying to gain entree into our crowd."

"But if they did sneak in, how would you handle it? Do rich people have goons?"

Bill frowned before laughing again. He had tried to stifle it but it didn't work. "You are so much fun."

I smiled sweetly and waited for him to continue.

He leaned in like he had a big secret to tell. "Rich people absolutely have goons. And they don't come cheap."

I leaned in too, and smiled slyly. "Have you ever had to dispatch a goon to handle business for you?"

"I'm afraid I can't tell you that. It's classified," he said with a wink.

All in all, it was a productive outing. I had more work to do on that front but step one of my plan was complete.

I got home and went straight to Farrah's room to check on her. Felicia had been there at some point; the scent of her favorite body lotion lingered in the air. Cucumber melon. So basic.

"Hey, beautiful! How are you feeling?" I asked.

Farrah shrugged. "Y'all need to stop fussing over me. I'm fine, I swear."

"Okay. Just checking. I'm gonna go take a nap."

"You got a package in the mail, by the way," she called after me.

Sure enough, a big white box with a gold bow sat on the coffee table. It was too pristine to have gone through the mail.

I slid the envelope out from under the bow and tore it open.

Mani,

This was supposed to be your birthday present but given the status of our relationship at this point, I wasn't sure if I'd see you then. I hope you enjoy this. Let it propel you into your future. It's bright, baby girl. Just keep believing in yourself.

Shawn

I hadn't had a chance to think about Shawn. Farrah and Bill had taken up all of my free time. And it was probably for the best because I had lost all my common sense behind the peen. Letting him hit raw? Bad move, really bad. I knew better but I got dickmatized. I was halfway to that raft in the ocean.

But now? Wrench in the plan. My birthday was in two weeks. How long had he been planning for it? He was more thoughtful than I knew. I felt my resolve crumbling.

I tore into the paper like a kid on Christmas morning. Inside was what looked to be a photo album. I frowned as I opened the cover but my confusion didn't last. It quickly turned to joy.

The inside cover read "Emerson Family Tree." There was a handwritten note inside from a Dr. Lisa Redding.

Emerson Family,

This book is the culmination of my careful research into your family's history. Share this with one another and fill in the blanks with photos, memories, and love. And remember, this is only the beginning!

I was speechless. And then the tears came. I couldn't believe he did this. He must have ordered it shortly after we met. It was a deeply personal gift, the kind of gift you give someone you care about.

I flipped through the book as if the pages were on fire. Names I had never heard, places I had never been, and photos I had never seen filled the first half. The second half was blank, ready for my family to fill with our own facts.

It was beautiful.

I picked up my phone and went to dial Shawn's number but I changed my mind. A gift this nice deserved a proper thank you.

<u>35</u>

Shawn

I stopped by Pop's office on my way out. It was an average workday aside from the fact that I couldn't stop thinking about Imani. Again.

I'd been useless the entire day. I was busy, but not with work. I checked my phone every five minutes, checked my email every thirty even though she's never emailed me before. I checked Top Shelf a few times just to see if her light was on. It wasn't. She hadn't blocked me, though, so maybe that was a good sign.

Lunch was a great distraction. DJ's kids were headed back to school next week so he took them to lunch downtown and they invited me to tag along. Kayla was six, Jared was eight, and Cameron was eleven, and I love those babies like they're my own.

It was fun, listening to them talk about the upcoming school year and seeing their friends again. The excitement--except for Cameron, who was at the "I hate school" stage--was contagious and I gave them each a $100 bill. DJ hates when I do that because he's always lecturing them about money and the value of a dollar. I get it, I guess, but I'm the uncle. I get to spoil them if I want to.

What would my life have been like if I had kids right now? I thought Tashka and I would have kids. I wanted four, she wanted two. That would have been cool. Oh, well.

Once I got back to work, my mood soured again.

The door to Pop's office was open but I knocked anyway. "You busy Pop?"

He looked busy but then he had always been good at giving the illusion that he was swamped. But I knew better. Because once, just once, I had caught him slipping. He had bellowed to Dita that he was in the middle of something and not to be disturbed but he let me in the office and I saw what was on his laptop: Solitaire.

"Come on," he said. "Any news from Al?"

I couldn't tell if this was his way of taking the assignment away from DJ and giving it to me or if he had forgotten he hadn't assigned it to me in the first place. The latter was a worse-case scenario for me. Pop had been forgetting more and more details lately.

I took a seat and set my bag in the chair next to me. "That's DJ, Pop. He's the one who's supposed to be talking to Al."

Pop looked at me like I was an idiot. "I know that."

"Okay..."

"Did you want something?"

"I just wanted to check in on you, old man. See you you're doing."

"I'm fine. Just busy," he said as he fiddled with the keys on his laptop. "You coming over for dinner tonight?"

My mother still cooked a couple of nights a week. It was her way of staying grounded. Plus, she enjoyed it. It was a past-time for southern women. "What's she making?"

"Now that, I do not know."

"Maybe. DJ and them coming?"

"I haven't talked to him. I'm sure if I invite him, he'll be there. Although the last thing he needs to be worrying about is food."

I'm not sure if it was the lingering frustration over Imani or my being fed up with Pop's relentless passive aggressive assaults on my big brother but I'd had it. "Do me a favor, Pop. Don't throw jabs at DJ when I'm around. If you have something to say to him, leave me out of it please."

I braced myself for the fallout. Pop took off his glasses and rubbed his eyes. He seemed tired but sur-prisingly, he didn't seem angry. "I respect that. I know you love your brother. You're loyal to him. I truly re-spect that."

"Then why do you do it?"

"Because I don't respect him."

"Why not?"

A strange thing happened just then. Pop rose from the big chair and walked around the side of his desk. He picked up my bag and set it on the floor before taking his seat next to me. "You wanna know?"

Oh, shit. Was he really about to tell me? I tried not to sound too eager. "I do."

"You really wanna know?"

"Pop, I really wanna know."

Pop took a deep breath and looked me dead in my eyes. "Tashka."

I frowned and stared at him in confusion. "Tashka? What does she have to do with anything?"

He sighed and shook his head. "Ask your brother."

<u>36</u>

Imani

With exactly three weeks left in my count-down, I took stock of my situation as it was. I had more cash than I ever had, but almost a third of it went toward getting my car fixed. The truth of the matter was that I was not gonna be able to pay my tuition at the rate I was going.

If one were so inclined, I suppose one could argue that I compromised my principals in order to reach my goal. It could also be argued that I let my guard down because I was finally healing from the past, and was therefore finally able to let a man in. Or there could be some third interpretation that's equally reductive.

The truth is...it was probably a combination of factors. But whatever it was that brought me there, I found myself standing at Shawn's door with the beautiful white leather-bound book in my arms.

A woman answered the door, someone I'd never seen before. She was short and homely, but she had a sweet smile and air about her. "Can I help you?" she asked. I looked down and saw that she had a feather duster in her hands.

"Is Shawn home?" I remembered my manners. "Sorry, I'm Imani. Nice to meet you."

The woman smiled. "I'm Lucille. Mr. Jeter is out. Would you like to leave a message? I'll make sure to get it to him."

I shifted the heavy book to redistribute the weight and give my arms some relief. Leave a message? No, I needed to say this in person. "Uhhhh...that's okay. I'll come back later."

I turned to walk away. Lucille called after me, "Ms. Imani?"

I whirled around. "Yes?"

"Would you like to come in and wait? I'm sure Mr. Jeter won't mind."

That's exactly what I did.

I sat in the foyer with the book on my lap. Lucille brought me a cup of tea (she insisted) and I declined a sandwich. She seemed to enjoy fussing over me but I wasn't in the mood today. I only had one thing on my mind.

Almost two hours later, Shawn finally came home. He entered through the garage door and I heard his voice before I saw him. It was the most comforting sound. He and Lucille had a muffled conversation and then he finally turned the corner. He looked upset but when he saw me, he seemed to relax. He didn't smile, but he did look pleased.

I stood. "I got something in the mail today."

He dropped his keys on the table. "Oh yeah?"

"Yeah. Shawn...it's beautiful. I can't believe you did this for me."

"I didn't do it, exactly. I hired someone to do it. Dr. Redding. She's very discreet if that's what you're worried about."

"I'm not worried. I'm grateful."

He shrugged. "I haven't seen it so don't worry about me knowing all your family business. She did the work and shipped it directly from her office. And--"

"Shawn! I don't care about that. I wanted to thank you in person."

"Well...you're welcome."

This was weird. Our little reunion wasn't going the way I'd hoped. "Is something wrong?"

He sat on the bench and his shoulders sagged, like he was bearing the weight of the world. "I got a lot on my mind. Got some bad news today."

I nodded. "That sucks," I said awkwardly. "You wanna talk about it?"

"Not really." He rubbed his forehead. He looked older than I remembered. Whatever he'd heard, it must have been bad.

"Look," he said, "I'm glad you liked your gift and I appreciate you coming to thank me in person."

"And?"

He raised his eyebrows and stared blankly. "And it's been a long day."

"Is that your way of asking me to leave?"

Shawn leaned back and rested his head against the wall as if the very act of speaking to me was making him tired. And then he broke my heart. "I ain't asking you for shit. Ever again."

My heart sank as I realized where Shawn's head was at. With nothing left to say, I simply turned and walked out. And I told myself I would never find myself back here again.

37

Imani couldn't have come by at a worse time. I had just gotten some news that sent me reeling. I wasn't exactly sure what it meant, yet, but I had a pretty good idea. And if I'm right, it explains every-thing.

I got home to find her in my foyer looking just as beautiful as ever. And judging by the look on her face, it seemed like that last wall had finally come down. But I wasn't in the right headspace to receive her. I probably should have just told her that. I'm sure she would have understood. Instead, I pushed her away.

I sat on the bench, right in the spot I'd found her in, and I could still smell her perfume. Part of me wanted to go after her, but the other part of me was too tired do the dance again. She was never going to change her mind and I for damn sure wasn't going to change mine.

Lucille came in with her bucket and mop. She was old school with her cleaning and I didn't mind that. She looked at me, looked away, then seemed to decide she had something to say.

"What is it?" I asked her.

"Ms. Imani. I like her," she said with a big smile.

"Yeah, me too." But it didn't matter now, did it?

"I took care of her while she waited. She wasn't hungry but I got her some tea."

So? "Okay. Thank you," I said, real close to being annoyed.

"She waited two hours for you," she said as she swept around my feet. "We talked a little bit."

"What did she say?"

"Well first, we talked about me. She asked me how long I worked for you, if I like it here, if I thought about going to school."

I wanted to be annoyed by that but instead, it brought a smile to my face. "What did you tell her?"

"I told her I like working for you, Mr. Jeter. I promise."

"It's okay. I hope you have higher aspirations than me."

Lucille chuckled. "I do want to go back to school one day. Ms. Imani gave me her number in case I need any advice about college."

"What would you go for?"

Lucille shrugged and leaned on the mop. "I've always had a mind for business."

"You never told me that."

"You never asked," she said with a grin.

It was true, I had never asked. Lucille resumed mopping and I stood to walk to my bedroom. I heard

Lucille's voice behind me. "She also said you were a good man and she's never known anybody like you."

Shit. What the hell am I doing?

I did an about-face and tucked my shirt back in. I went to grab my keys and didn't see them, but when I turned around to retrace my steps, Lucille was standing there with my keys and a huge grin. "What's her favorite meal?"

I grabbed the keys and laughed at Lucille as I headed out, calling back to her, "tell him she likes truffle fries."

38

Imani

I finally reached Fran when I was halfway to my apartment. I could hear little Andrew crying in the background when she picked up.

I told her about Shawn and the family tree and the fact that he basically put me out of his house. I was expecting her to say I told you so but she spared me.

"Well, listen, there are other fish in the water. Just count it as a lesson and keep pushing. Right?"

"I guess," I said, but I didn't really agree.

"If I didn't know any better, I'd think you have real feelings for this one."

"Maybe. But that's not why I called you. It's about Farrah."

"Oh yeah, how's she doing?"

"Physically, she's okay. Emotionally, I think she's still got a long way to go."

"Did they ever catch the guy?"

"No. And that's what I'm calling you about. You once told me you have a friend who's a private investigator."

She was quiet for a minute. "Why are you asking?"

"It's all above board, Fran. I wanna retain your friend, that's all. If I'm gonna keep doing this, I need my own vetting system, you know what I mean? I don't want me or Farrah going through something like this again."

"That's smart. Okay, yeah. I'll text you her info when we get off the phone."

"Cool, thank you."

Fran laughed. "I think you have a future in this."

"In what?"

"Sugaring."

"Just until I get my tuition money. Then I'm done."

"You say that. It was easy money, wasn't it?"

"I wouldn't call it easy but I kinda like doing it."

"And you're good at it. Natural talent."

I laughed. "I don't think so."

Someone behind me honked once. Then they honked again. Then they leaned on their horn, which was odd because I hadn't done anything wrong. I checked my rearview mirror and was shocked to see Shawn behind me.

"Let me call you back," I told Fran. I ended the call and pulled over in the parking lot of a Bank of America. Shawn pulled in behind me and got out of his car. I glanced at the white book on my passenger seat and waited.

I rolled the window down before he could

knock. He looked different. More like his usual self. "What do you want, Shawn?"

"I wanted to tell you I'm sorry for how I acted back there. It's been a rough day but I should have never taken it out on you."

"You're right. You shouldn't have. Anything else?"

"You gon' make me do this outside?"

Without answering, I hit the button to unlock the door and he walked around and got in the passenger seat. He placed the book on his lap and turned to face me. "Why did you come see me?"

He looked so good. It was hard to concentrate. "I told you, I wanted to thank you in person. The gift was...it was perfect. So thank you."

"That's all you wanted to say?"

I stared straight ahead and pretended to think about it. I wanted him to sweat just a little while longer before I gave in.

Finally, I turned to look at him. My handsome knight. "I also wanted to say I'm in."

He smiled, just a little, like he was being cautious. "Meaning...?"

"I wanna be with you. Let's get on that raft together."

"Are you sure? Even--"

"Even if it means giving up my profile. Yes. I'm sure."

He leaned in and grabbed my face before pressing his lips softly against mine. I kissed him back hungrily, damn near ready to take my clothes off then and there. But Shawn pulled away before we got too carried away. "Let's go to my place," he said. "Otherwise I'mma throw you in the backseat."

"Notice I'm not disagreeing with that."

He looked around. "Bank of America, huh? Is that a hint?"

"Shut up!" I said, hitting him playfully. "About that, though--"

"Mani, I meant what I said. I wanna take care of you. I *got* you. Whatever you need. Whatever you want."

"Right now, I want you."

"You got me, baby. I'm yours."

And that was that.

Later on, after we made love, we lay in his bed, hugged up and in the bliss of our new relationship. I wasn't completely sure where we were headed. After all, there were still a few issues to sort through. I didn't want my family to know. He had his father to deal with, along with something serious going on with his brother and their company. And I needed to make sure Mr. Andretti paid for what he did. After that, I wanted to hook Farrah up with one of Shawn's friends. And then, of course, my classes were to start in three weeks. This was gonna be an interesting senior year.

But for now, there was only sleep, which I did in the arms of my billionaire boyfriend.

Epilogue

It had been an amazing two weeks. Shawn and I had spent almost every waking moment together. Eating, drinking, laughing, partying and having sex. And with my tuition paid in full, I was able to relax and enjoy those moments without worrying about the future. As far as I was concerned, my future was on the upswing. Life was *good*.

My new private investigator, Donna Kemp, was officially on retainer. She'd found Mr. Andretti's information--his real name was Jacob Rasmussen--and the plan was in motion. The police were taking their good old time finding him so it just made sense to take matters into my own hands. Shawn didn't know anything about this, and he didn't need to know. My profile was down and I was done with sugaring.

For the most part. I had plans to keep one foot in the game. Shawn didn't need to know that either.

Daddy was doing much better. He still wasn't at one hundred percent but he didn't need to be. I was approaching a point where I'd be able to supplement Mama's income.

With classes one week away and my textbooks already ordered, I took a day to pamper myself. I was at the nail salon with my feet in hot water as the chair massaged my back when I got a phone call. Ugh, it was Giovanni.

I debated letting it go to voicemail but then I thought about it. He never calls me. What if it was an emergency? What if something was wrong with my daddy?

"Hey Giovanni."

"Hey, big sister. What you up to?"

He sounded strange. Like he had a secret to tell. I proceeded cautiously. "I'm getting my nails done. Did you need something?"

"Kind of. I have a question."

"Okay," I said, bored already.

"I'm about to send you a text."

"That's not a question."

"Look at the picture first."

I rolled my eyes and looked at my screen, hoping the picture came right through. I didn't have time for this shit.

There it was. I clicked the pic and enlarged it to full screen. It appeared to be a picture of a crowd of people. "Yeah, it came through. What is this?"

"Jade sent it to me. You remember Jade?"

"One of your little friends? Why would I?"

He snickered. "She follows all these gossip blogs and that pic was on the Shaderoom. It's from Drake's party at Lighthouse."

Shit. My heart began to pound. "What about it?"

"Look in the upper right corner. Is that you sitting next to Michael B Jordan?"

I'm screwed.

Imani, Shawn, and the whole crew will be back in book 2:
A Billionaire Decision

If you enjoyed this novel, please consider
leaving a review on Amazon or Goodreads
so other readers can enjoy it, too!

About the Author

Shae Sanders grew up sneaking her sister's Jackie Collins novels when she really didn't have any business reading them. But they stoked a love of edgy and steamy romance against the backdrop of business and power. In her spare time, Shae watches her favorite shows over and over again.

Books By Shae Sanders

Novellas
First Class Love
Love and War

Series

<u>Candy Girls</u>
My Billionaire Benefactor (Candy Girls Book 1)
A Billionaire Decision (Candy Girls Book 2)
My Billionaire Holiday: A Novella
(Candy Girls Book 3)
Their Billionaire Secrets (Candy Girls Book 4)
A Billionaire Ending (Candy Girls Book 5) *coming soon*

<u>Hailey Family</u>
The Boyfriend Type
The Playbook